HELL TO PAY

By
Robert Fisher

La Maison Publishing, Inc.
Vero Beach, Florida
The Hibiscus City
lamaisonpublishing@gmail.com

Chapter 1

Hunter and Prey

Late in the evening, Sister Claire Darcy walked through the streets of Malvara on her way back to the Convent. The small town, located in the Columbian jungle, was preparing for a peaceful evening among the verdant fauna of the Amazon. Sister Darcy was a tall, attractive woman with pale skin and red hair; she was wearing the black and white habit of a Catholic nun. Her appearance and height made her very recognizable among the town's people. Unlike some of the other sisters in her Convent, most of which had come from the big cities in Northern

Colombia, Sister Darcy hailed from Belfast in Northern Ireland.

She loved the peaceful town and its people but most importantly because it was in the middle of nowhere and was isolated from the rest of the world and her past. She especially loved walking around the town taking in cool nights, when the trees and buildings were silhouetted against the waning light of day. Counting Claire, there were four nuns in the Convent Sister Garcia, Sister Luna, and Mother Lucrezia, who oversaw the Convent's activities and day-to-day operations. Garcia and Luna were the youngest at twenty-five and twenty-six respectively while Mother Lucrezia was the oldest at sixty-seven while Claire was thirty-eight. As the second oldest nun at the convent, Claire had become a kind of big sister for Sister Garcia and Sister Luna.

Her current life was a far cry from the life she led before coming to the Convent, and she enjoyed it immensely. She walked past the market and waved at the owner of one of the fruit stands as he was closing up his shop. He was a kindly old man who had lived in Malvara his entire life.

"Hola Senor Santos" she called out warmly in her quiet Irish accent. The man looked back at her and returned the gesture; one of the few benefits of her former life was that she had mastered numerous other languages.

"Hola Hermana Darcy" said the man smiling as she kept walking.

Many of the villagers there knew her.

A few minutes later, she arrived at the Convent. Sister Garcia was standing with a broom on the steps of the Convent. She was a short young girl who had come to the convent from Bogota. She looked up at Sister Darcy and smiled. "Hola Hermana," she said warmly.

"Hello, Sister Garcia. How are you this evening?"

"Fine. Mother Lucrezia wanted me to do some sweeping," answered Sister Garcia.

"Good, I'll help you," said Sister Darcy smiling.

She walked up the steps and into the Convent, opened the broom closet and grabbed a broom then walked back out to join Sister Garcia.

"Where is Sister Luna?" asked Claire as she began sweeping.

"She's with Mother Lucrezia at the homeless shelter," answered Garcia. "They'll be back later," she continued as they kept on sweeping.

Claire smiled subtly. The four of them were like a family; she often wondered if she deserved such a family. The Catholic Convent, where they lived and worked was built by Spanish conquistadors centuries ago as a garrison and was then converted into a Convent by missionaries. It was named the First Convent of Saint Mary, and behind it was the town cemetery. The Convent was located at the edge of Malvara along a dirt road. It was where Claire had begun her search for redemption three years ago.

"Good, is it my turn to make dinner tonight?" asked Claire.

Sister Garcia nodded in answer.

"I'll go get it started," said Claire with a smile. She walked inside the convent, while Sister Garcia continued to clean the front steps.

As she made her way to the kitchen, she could still remember when she first came to the convent. It was a rainy night. She had come begging for help and salvation. Mother Lucrezia took her in promising to help her find forgiveness in the eyes of God for which she was eternally grateful. She hated having to deceive those who had taken her in by using a fake name and identity but it was necessary in case someone came looking for her. She wanted nothing to do with her past— the only evidence of who she was lay in locked chest under her bed and was tattooed across her back.

*****

"Somebody, wake him up!" barked the Police Captain gruffly in his thick Texan accent as he gestured angrily to the man with his head down on the table. The sleeping man had unkempt shoulder length brown hair and pale skin. He was dressed in a short light brown trench coat, a white dress shirt with a red tie and dark grey pants; his face was slightly unshaven since he had been too busy to shave. Upon hearing the Captains orders, the man lifted his head wearily off of the table.

"You don't have to yell, Captain. This isn't Rogers Centre," said the man as he rubbed his eyes.

The mobile command center of the Corpus Christi police department sat not far from its target. The walls of the inside were crammed with corkboards and monitors lining the side and technicians seated behind desks were typing away at computers.

"If you don't like how I do things, Agent Mendelsohn, then you can leave," said the Captain brusquely.

"I'm afraid you're not that lucky," said Barry Mendelsohn dryly as he stood up and walked towards the coffee machine behind him, ignoring the Captain's attitude.

The Captain was a large older man in his late forties with a thick gray mustache under his nose. He had a stern face and demeanor as well as an imperious personality.

"And speaking of which, Captain, I have been tracking these people all the way from Ottawa for the last three weeks," said Mendelsohn as he picked up a paper cup next to the coffee maker.

"Now as I recall your superiors instructed you to listen to me and heed my wisdom regarding these two," he continued as he lifted up the coffee pot and poured its black contents into the cup.

"Personally I'd rather be back in Canada, but my superiors at Interpol instructed me to find these guys and cooperate with local law enforcement to capture them so I can extradite them back to Ottawa before they can escape to Mexico," said Barry as he poured sugar and cream into the coffee and proceeded to stir it with a plastic spoon until it turned brown.

He took a long gulp of the coffee and shivered ever so slightly as the hot liquid poured down his throat. Having gotten his drink he lowered the coffee and shifted his attention to the Captain.

"Now it is clear to me that you and me don't like each other but we have a job to do, so if it's all the same to you can we end this dick measuring contest and get on with it?" asked Barry before taking another sip of the coffee.

The Captain glared at him, unaccustomed to being spoken to in such a way and not approving of it either.

"Fine" glared the Captain.

"Excellent…. Are your men in position?" asked Barry.

"I have a four man SWAT team positioned right outside the safe house," said the Captain as he pointed to one of the screens. "And another four positioned not far behind as back up," continued the Captain as he pointed to another screen.

Barry glanced at the screens and saw footage from each of the officer's body cameras. "Is this even necessary for just two Mexicans?" asked the Captain smugly.

"These two Mexicans are hit men for the Sinaloa Cartel and they're responsible for killing two Interpol agents in Ottawa among others so…yes any more questions?" asked Barry annoyed at the question.

"Is there anything else I should know about them before I send my men in?" asked the Captain.

"Nothing that I didn't tell you at the briefing," answered Barry.

The Captain grinned ever so slightly and picked up his two-way radio. "Begin your insertion, team one," said the Captain.

Barry watched the screen as the officers cautiously approached the small house at the end of the street. Suddenly a barrage of automatic gunfire echoed from one of the windows, causing everyone in the command center to jump.

The SWAT officers immediately took cover behind a car as the shooters continued firing at them. One of them tossed a tear gas grenade through the window of the house before quickly jumping back into cover. Within seconds, a cloud of thick white gas began to emanate from the windows followed by coughing. Seizing their opportunity, the SWAT officers quickly donned their gas masks, ran inside the house, and arrested the two men. Those inside the command center watched as the officers walked the two men out the front door of the house in handcuffs.

"Looks like you'll be going back to Canada with your friends after all," said the Captain with an arrogant smirk across his face.

"Can't wait," Barry replied dryly with a light smile on his face. At that moment, his cellphone began to ring loudly.

"Give me a second," said Barry as he pulled his cellphone out of his pocket and answered it.

"Hello?" said Barry. After a pause. "Yes Sir, what is the problem?"

While Barry listened to the voice on the other end of the phone as the Captain watched curiously as the grin on Barry's face slowly changed to a frown.

"I understand Sir, I'll be on the first flight to Lyon" said Barry just as the call ended.

Barry returned the phone to his pocket and shrugged with a disappointed, annoyed look on his face.

"What was that all about?" asked the Captain.

"It looks like I'm not going home after all," said Barry dismissively.

Chapter 2

Devil Woman

It had been raining on the Fuerzas Armadas Revolucionarias de Columbia camp for around two hours now. Colloquially known as FARC and known to the world as the Revolutionary Armed Forces of Columbia-People's Army, the Marxist terrorist group had been at war with the Columbian government for decades. The leader of the camp, Front Commander Sandoval, lay asleep on a cot in the command tent. Outside the camp was a hive of activity as his men raced around the camp either hiding from the rain or preparing for the upcoming operation. If you looked up and squinted, you would see a small barely visible black dot circling the camp in the dying orange light of the evening. Many of the men would occasionally look up and scowl at it knowing all too well, what it was. The men were tired, having spent weeks on the run from government forces, yet they had faith in their commander's promise that this would soon end.

Suddenly the commander's sleep was interrupted by one of his lieutenants, a young man from the slums of Barranquilla. Groggily the commander rose from his cot and rubbed his face, the lieutenant's excitement drowned out the content of his words.

"Paolo!" barked the Commander.

The Lieutenant abruptly stopped speaking and stood at attention in response. "Start over, what's going on?" said Sandoval.

The Lieutenant took a deep breath before speaking: "Sir, we have visitors… and they insist on speaking to you."

Must be our friends from Cuba here with the weapons they promised us, he thought as he picked up a cup of water from the stand next to his bed and took a sip. "Cubans?" he asked casually rubbing the filth of sleep from his eyes.

"No Sir," replied Paolo.

"I see," said Sandoval as he stood up washed his face with a towel from a nearby washbasin. Must be SEBIN agents with supplies from Venezuela reasoned Sandoval as he finished washing his bearded face. It was an apt assumption since the Venezuelan intelligence agency had been a supporter of FARC's for years.

"Venezuelans?" he asked.

"No sir…Gringos," answered the lieutenant.

Surprised he looked at the young lieutenant. "Gringos?" asked Sandoval.

"Yes sir," replied Paolo.

Sandoval raised his eyebrow, curious at this development. He grabbed his black beret with a single red star on the front of it and put it on.

"Well…let's go see what they want," he said smugly as he walked out of the tent.

Paolo followed him. The two men saw parked in the middle of the camp a black Escalade EVS with a black military Hummer behind it. Standing in front of the Escalade were three men holding futuristic looking rifles guarding a man in a black trench coat with a large fedora carrying a briefcase that was handcuffed to his wrist. His guards wore black military fatigues, their faces hidden by balaclavas so that only their eyes were visible. Sandoval's men, desperate looking jungle guerillas, stared at them. Some were aiming their AK-47 assault rifles at the three men, who ignored them.

As Sandoval walked up to him, the man in the fedora had a pleased grin on his face.

"How pleasant it is to finally meet you, Commander Sandoval," said the man in the fedora casually and in flawless Spanish.

Sandoval could not place the man's accent; it was cold and lifeless, impossible to determine its origin.

"You have come a long way to die," Sandoval replied in Spanish.

The man in the fedora laughed softly. His reaction surprised Sandoval and his men.

"Commander, if you kill us you will be killing yourselves," said the man.

"Explain," grunted Sandoval.

The man pointed up with his index finger at a barely visible drone in the sky.

"That drone is controlled by my people, and inside that drone are two Hellfire missiles capable of leveling this entire camp, if need be," answered the man. "I think it would benefit everyone here if my people don't see a need to use them, don't you?" he continued.

His icy tone told Sandoval that he wasn't bluffing. He motioned to his men to lower their rifles, which they did. "What do you want?" he asked.

"Merely to talk… in private," said the man in the fedora.

Sandoval nodded and motioned to the tent.

"Excellent," said the man as he followed Sandoval into the tent.

Once inside they sat down at a small table. The man placed his briefcase on the table and tented his fingers on top of it with Sandoval sitting across from him.

"Who are you?" Sandoval asked.

"For simplicities sake call me Nelec, I am a representative of an organization that has certain… interests in this region. Interests that would be jeopardized by your planned offensive," explained Nelec.

How do they know Sandoval wondered?

"I can see that you are surprised that we know. Rest assured that none of your men are spies... it was the most logical move given your history," said Nelec.

"However my superiors have a counter proposal that would benefit everyone. The base you plan to attack is prepared and will massacre you and your men. This is not an opinion but hard fact.

"However, not far from here is a small easily defensible town called Malvara that you and your people could easily take and fortify against the government forces that would surely come after you.

"My superiors are prepared to reward you handsomely if you make this change," concluded Nelec.

"We are not mercenaries," growled Sandoval, angry at the insinuation.

"Spare me the politics, Commander. The FARC has signed a peace treaty with the government and disarmed, while you and your men are one of the few groups still willing to fight a war everyone in this country would like to forget," replied Nelec. "It's pathetic really."

"I've killed men for speaking to me like that," growled Sandoval.

"Need I remind you of what will happen if you try to kill me?" Nelec replied, unfazed by Sandoval's simmering anger.

The two men glared at each other for a minute unsure of what to say. Finally, Nelec reached into his coat pocket, pulled out a key, and used it to unlock the cuffs around his wrist. He stood up and rubbed his now free wrist.

"Inside are maps of the area and plans for the attack and everything else you will need to take Malvara and see that I'm right. The choice is yours, Commander," said Nelec as he walked out of the tent.

"Just know that we will be watching you," said Nelec before walking out.

Once he was gone, Sandoval cautiously opened the briefcase, ignoring the sound of Nelec and his men driving away. Carefully he looked over the papers and maps and saw that his plan was right. What angered him most though was that Nelec was also right about him and the FARC but with the right support and backing, Nelec's "superiors" could help him in return. He sighed and walked out of the tent and greeted Paolo.

"Sir, who was that man?" asked Paolo.

"Never mind….have you ever heard of a town called Malvara?" Sandoval asked.

*****

The International Criminal Police Organization, commonly known as either Interpol, or by its acronym ICPO, is headquartered inside an unimpressive square shaped building beside the Rhone River in Lyon, France. It is a state-of-the-art facility dedicated to assisting the worlds various law enforcement agencies. According to its charter, Interpol agents are not allowed to make arrests. They mostly assist local law enforcement in the pursuit and apprehension of criminals, terrorists, and fugitives. The organization has offices in countries all over the world.

The building had a certain imperious glow to it in the bright sunlight of the afternoon. Barry Mendelsohn welcomed the warmer climate, greatly preferring it to his frigid Canadian homeland. As his car pulled up to the building, he straightened his tie. It wasn't the first time Mendelsohn had been there but it was the first time that he had been summoned by the Director of Interpol himself. He ran his hands though his hair and took a deep breath.

Standing outside of the building was a French woman in a suit. As Mendelsohn got out of the car, the woman walked up to him and they shook hands.

She greeted him," Welcome to Lyon, Agent Mendelsohn. The Director is expecting you."

"I would hope so," said Mendelsohn.

"Now, you come with me," replied the woman dryly as she turned and began walking inside.

Mendelsohn shrugged and followed her; still curious as to why he had been summoned. Upon entering the building, they were stopped by two security guards. Mendelsohn, knowing exactly what they were going to request, reached into the shoulder holster under his coat and pulled out his pistol, a Beretta 8000 Cougar F. Politely he handed it to the two guards who disappeared into a security room. The woman looked at him quizzically. "You know we don't carry guns, right?" she asked.

Barry nodded, "I only use it for emergencies," he replied with a smirk.

The woman shrugged and motioned for him to follow her across the lobby to an elevator.

After a quick ride up, they arrived at the top floor. They walked down a long hallway and then through a door at the end of the hall. Mendelsohn wasn't surprised at how busy the various personnel were. In addition to serving as Interpol's headquarters for various bureaucratic reasons, it also served as the linchpin of Interpol's global criminal database. The database contained information on the world's most dangerous criminals, making it an invaluable asset to various law enforcement agencies across the globe.

They entered a small office; there was a couch against the wall and an empty desk next to a door with a sign on it that read: Director Harvey Lohman. Mendelsohn was about to sit on the couch, when the woman spoke.

"Go inside. He's waiting," she said.

Mendelsohn nodded in understanding, opened the door, and walked in. The Director's office was a spacious room with bookcases on the left and right walls. In the middle of the room, sitting behind a wooden desk with two chairs in front of it, was the Director himself.

The desk was nowhere near as cluttered as he had expected. Besides the usual office supplies that were neatly organized on the desk, there was a file stamped CLASSIFIED in red capital letters. Mendelsohn's curiosity as to why he had been summoned here grew upon seeing the folder. Director Lohman was an older man of about fifty with glasses and a growing bald spot. He was wearing a dark blue suit with a blue vest, a white dress shirt, and tie.

His demeanor reminded him of the principal at his elementary school. When Mendelsohn walked in, Lohman looked up from a file he was reading marked B Mendelsohn.

"Ah, you're here, Welcome Agent Mendelsohn. Please sit down," said Lohman as he gestured graciously to the chairs in front of the desk.

Mendelsohn nodded; glad to be treated politely. He walked over to one of the chairs and sat down. Lohman closed the file he was reading and placed it on the desk, before adjusting his glasses.

"I was just reviewing your file, Agent Mendelsohn. You had quite the interesting life before joining us," said Lohman. "You were born in the city of Toronto and spent five years in the Canadian army, followed by three years in the Canadian Security Intelligence Service CSIS before joining Interpol, is that right?" he asked.

Barry nodded curious as to where this was going.

"I'm curious, why did you leave the CSIS for Interpol?" asked Lohman.

"Is this some kind of performance review or something?" wondered Mendelsohn. Best to go along with whatever this is, he thought.

"The short version is that I felt I could do more good at Interpol than in the CSIS," answered Mendelsohn.

"I see," said Lohman ponderously and glanced back at the classified file on his desk.

"Pardon me sir, but what is the purpose of this meeting?" asked Mendelsohn.

Lohman's eyes darted up from the files to Mendelsohn. Then he leaned back in his chair, looking like he had just come to a decision.

"Alright then, I have a special assignment I want you to undertake for me," answered Lohman.

Mendelsohn sighed, feeling relieved at having his question answered, though his curiosity had been aroused as to what this special assignment could be.

"Three months ago, we intercepted a high priority message from the Heise She Li Triad to their agents across the world," said Lohman.

"What was the message, sir?" asked Mendelsohn.

"Frankly, it's the reason why we called you in," said Lohman. He picked a piece of paper off his desk and handed it to Mendelsohn.

Mendelsohn proceeded to read the message on the paper.

All personnel—be on the lookout for this woman.

Name: Siobhan Costello.
AKA The Devil Woman.
Born: Belfast, Northern Ireland.
Height: Six feet, three inches
Eyes: Green
Hair: Red and long
Age: Between 35 and 40

Former assassin for a splinter faction of the Irish Republican Army, referred to itself as The IRA. Be advised she is extremely dangerous, capture only. Killing her will result in severe punishment. Is skilled in multiple martial arts including Adithada, Arnis, Aikido, Savate, Baguazhang, Yaw-Yan, Ninjutsu, Boxing, Krav Maga, Kyudo, Judo, Wing Chun, Capoeira, Francombat, Hapkido,

Shorin-ryu, Chin Na, Hung Gar, Kickboxing, Jeet Kune Do, Shaolin, Kung Fu, Kenpo, Taekwondo, Kenjitsu, Hapkido, Muay Thai, Escrima, Karate, Silat, Russian Sambo, Systema, and Asgarda.

Tattooed across her back are the words: Erin go Bragh (Ireland Forever).

Expert with all NATO and WARSAW Pact firearms, knife throwing and guerilla tactics.

Below was a photo of a beautiful tall woman with pale skin and an athletic, voluptuous body. She was dressed in green camo pants and a black tank top. She was wearing reflective aviator sunglasses while brandishing an AK-47. Her bright red hair was tied into a ponytail.

Around her forehead was a green camo headband.

"She almost looks like a model," remarked Mendelsohn as he studied the picture then handed the paper back to Lohman.

"Don't let her appearance fool you. She's one of the deadliest women on Earth," answered Lohman.

"Why is she called the Devil Woman?" asked Mendelsohn.

"Allegedly it's because of her bright red hair," answered Lohman.

"Why is the Triad interested in her?" asked Barry curiously.

"That's what we want you to find out," said Lohman.

Mendelsohn was not completely surprised at the answer.

"Pardon me, sir but why me?" asked Barry. "I'm not an expert on the Triad or the IRA, wouldn't it be easier to hire Mosaic to find her or notify the British and Irish governments?"

"Personally I distrust organizations like Mosaic and I'd prefer to keep this in house. As for notifying the Brits, well I don't think they'd take this seriously considering she's supposed to have been dead for the last three years," Lohman replied. "Besides you are an expert at finding people that don't want to be found, your recent mission to Texas being just one example," he continued.

Mendelsohn shrugged trying to think of a way out of this assignment when it occurred to him that something Lohman said didn't make sense.

"Sir, what do you mean she's been dead?" he asked confused.

"Six years ago she was part of an ultraviolent IRA splinter cell, terrorized the Brits for three years before trying to blow up Balmoral Castle with a car bomb."

"What happened?" asked Mendelsohn.

"The car bomb exploded prematurely with her in it, the body was too burned and disfigured for facial recognition," explained Lohman. "However they still declared her dead, since they had the blood type and dental records," he continued. "The whole story and more is in the dossier," said Lohman as he pointed at the folder in front of him.

"So what am I supposed to do exactly, sir?" asked Mendelsohn sensing an ulterior motive.

"You know as well as I do that the Heise She Li aren't your typical gangsters; they are far more precise and organized than that."

Despite his lack of experience with the Triad, Barry had read numerous reports from fellow Interpol agents regarding them. The reports mentioned a strong sense of discipline amongst its members. One document compared the demeanor of its enforcers and members—referred to in the Triad as Red Poles and 49ers respectively—to the military. Another said that its members resembled that of a Special Forces unit instead of mobsters. Even more impressive was that their reach extended well beyond their native Asia to across the globe with each outpost maintaining contact with the Triads leadership in Hong Kong as well as maintaining a massive intelligence network.

"The Triad obviously thinks she is still alive, which means they have gathered sufficient evidence to justify sending out a message to their people," answered Lohman. "I want you to find Costello and arrest her before the Triad can contact her."

"Do you think she is still alive, sir?" Barry asked.

"It doesn't matter what I think, an organization like the Heise She Li wouldn't go through all this trouble to find a dead woman," said Lohman bluntly. "If she's still alive then she has to pay for all the people she's killed and I'll take any chance I can to screw with the Heise She Li triad," he continued.

"Be that as it may, sir, I still need some kind of lead to start. Where would I even begin looking for her?" asked Mendelsohn.

Harvey Lohman sighed. "Unfortunately the trail has gone cold."

"However, we approached British intelligence about this and they contacted an MI6 agent that had a run-in with her years ago," explained Lohman. "He'll point you in the right direction," he said.

"I see. Well, who is he and where do I meet him?" asked Barry Mendelsohn.

"According to MI6 he's known as SABRE," answered Lohman.

Mendelsohn groaned quietly, he hated working with spies. He knew from personal experience that spies were hard to trust, not to mention the morally gray area that spies inhabited which is what drove him to quit the CSIS in the first place.

"You'll meet him in Hyde Park once you arrive in London," said Lohman ignoring Mendelsohn's barely audible groan.

"I see. Could this have anything to do with that firefight on Sankan Island three months ago?" asked Mendelsohn.

"We don't know, frankly I don't think anyone knows what that was about... and those that do are either dead or not talking," answered Lohman. "Hell, I wouldn't worry about that; anyway why do you ask?"

"I've been following it since it happened mostly out of curiosity."

"Like I said, don't worry about it, I have a team working on it but they haven't found anything useful and frankly I don't expect them to," answered Lohman.

Mendelsohn wasn't surprised at his answer. The Triad and the Vasilev Syndicate were experts at covering their tracks, and the fact that it was on Sankan Island made it practically impossible to conduct an investigation into it, since the Triad and the Vasilev Syndicate controlled the island.

"But we do know that the Rojas cartel was forced off the island by the Triad and the Syndicate. Anyway, back to the matter at hand, you're booked on the 3:00 flight to London," finished Lohman.

"Understood sir. I'll get going then," said Mendelsohn as he stood up.

"And be careful. I wasn't kidding when I said she was one of the most dangerous women on Earth," said Lohman as Mendelsohn walked to the door.

Mendelsohn turned to face Lohman, "Yes sir." With that, he walked out the door.

Chapter 3

The Temple

Siobhan had an exercise routine that she carried out early every morning when the sky was still dark and the town was still fast asleep. The routine began with one hundred push-ups and sit-ups followed by a jog around the town and ending with her practicing martial arts skills in a clearing in the woods.

She had already completed her push-ups and sit-ups and was walking quietly through the Convent so as not to awaken Sister Luna and Sister Garcia, who were asleep in their rooms. She was at the front door of the Convent when she suddenly felt like she was being watched.

"Going somewhere, Claire?" said a familiar voice behind her.

Instinctively she quickly turned around and was somewhat surprised to see Mother Lucrezia standing next to the pulpit. She had forgotten that Mother Superior woke up earlier than the rest of them.

Lucrezia was an old gray-haired Italian woman with a crackly authoritative accent. Despite her compassion, her eyes had the look of someone that had taken a life before. It was a look that reminded Siobhan of her time in the IRA where she was surrounded by killers fighting for a cause that was old when they were young.

"Just going outside for my exercise," answered Siobhan.

"I can see that," Mother Lucrezia replied gesturing to the cheap gray tracksuit Siobhan was wearing.

Siobhan felt as if she was in trouble for not wearing her habit. She had preferred to keep her morning ritual a secret from her sisters lest they suspect anything. She often asked herself why she kept up her old exercise regimen. She wondered if it was something, she was so used to be doing or more like a compulsion or a calling.

Whatever the reason, she couldn't help but feel nervous at being confronted by Mother Superior. She was about to speak when Lucrezia stopped her by holding up her hand.

"Do not feel ashamed my child; you will not offend the Lord if you wear that suit for your exercise," she said warmly.

Siobhan felt relieved and comforted at hearing Lucrezia's kind reassuring words.

"After all, your bodies are temples of the Holy Spirit," she continued.

"Therefore, honor God with your bodies, 1 Corinthians 6:19-20," replied Siobhan finishing the Bible verse.

"Very good, enjoy your run, Claire," said. Lucrezia impressed at her quotation.

Claire nodded and turned to the door, opened it and walked out. After stretching, she began jogging down the dirt road into the town. The sun had not yet begun to rise and the town was dark and quiet. The only light in the seemingly infinite darkness of the jungle town was from the streetlights, and the only sound in the intimidating endless quiet came from the animals in the jungle.

The temperature was cool and the wind was breezy and refreshing with the occasional gust cooling Siobhan's skin as she sweated during her run. In a way, Malvara in the early morning reminded her of the small villages in the Irish countryside she grew up in as a child — peaceful, calm and surrounded by the eternal greenery of nature. As she passed the market, she began to slow from a run to a brisk walk. Down the street from the market was Armando's, the only bar in Malvara. It was the only building with the lights on this early in Malvara.

Curiously, she stopped and looked inside through the window. The bartender was cleaning shot glasses and there were three men sitting on stools, passed out on the bar. Occasionally she and Mother Lucrezia would go into the bar and spread the word to the patrons, but most of them never listened because they were either drunk or passed out. Siobhan grinned at the sight and continued walking, again reminded of her Irish home.

Not far from Armando's was the town hall in the center of town. It was easily the largest building in town and it had seen better days. Its paint was chipped and there were cracks in the concrete but it served its purpose nonetheless. On the top of the building was a spire-like structure that seemed to stab the heavens. On top of the steeple was the Colombian flag that fluttered lightly in the gentle morning breeze. She passed the hall, resumed running and followed the main road, which led out of the town. Once she was out of the town, she took a left into the forest that surrounded the town like an infinite green wall, and jogged down a short path and up a small hill. At the top of the hill the path ended in a small clearing where she would practice her martial arts skills.

Not far from the clearing was a brook where she would get water to drink after practicing. In the middle of the clearing was a cart with a large sack of grain in it that served as her punching bag. Occasionally during her practice, she asked herself why she even continued to practice like this anymore. She was no longer a killer for the IRA and it had been years since she had to use her skills and — most importantly — the world and MI6 believed she was dead, so they were all but unnecessary. But despite all of those reasons and more she couldn't answer her own question.

Mother Lucrezia would often tell them that God's will manifested itself in mysterious ways and that we would find that out one day; but that always made her even more curious. She often asked herself — was it God preparing her for some great test of faith? A compulsion? Or was it that after years of training she had conditioned herself to engage in this morning ritual? Whatever the reason she found it therapeutic and cathartic nonetheless.

She sighed and walked over to the brook, knelt down, placed her hands in the brook and cupped some water in her hands and drank it. Feeling refreshed she walked back to the clearing and began stretching. When she was done stretching, she took a deep breath and cracked her knuckles.

Then suddenly she hit the bag with her fist, which was instantly followed by a barrage of blindingly fast kicks. She continued striking the bag and her speed gradually increased causing her arms and legs to resemble a blur. Some small part of her was impressed with herself that she could still hit as hard and fast as she did when she was in the IRA, though she would never admit it to anyone but herself. Over the next several hours she continued hitting and kicking the bag, occasionally stopping to use a nearby tree for pull-ups. The constant blows to the bag of grain had caused her hands to get sore and bruised but she had long since learned to ignore the pain.

Her practicing was interrupted by a ray of sunlight; she turned and saw the sun beginning to rise. She glanced at the battered bag; there were a few rips on it. Have to get a new one soon, she thought. She turned and began jogging back to the Convent. She grinned as she imagined the reactions of the boys in her school in her village in Ireland if they knew how deadly she was.

She reentered the town and noticed it was starting to stir to life, making it all the more important that she get home before anyone see her like this. When she returned to the Convent, Sister Luna and Sister Garcia were still asleep and would still be for a few more hours. Mother Lucrezia was nowhere to be seen; Siobhan assumed she was in her study. She walked back to her room and grinned, wondering how Sister Luna and Sister Garcia would react if they knew what mild mannered "Sister Claire Darcy" did in the morning while they were asleep. When she reached her room, she walked inside, closed the door, and removed her sweaty clothes and grabbed a towel to wipe the sweat off her body. Then she got into bed and fell asleep.

*****

Located under the River Thames in London rested the headquarters of England's elite black ops counterintelligence agency known as Equinox. Since Equinox received its orders from the Prime Minister and was a subsidiary of MI6, it was strategically positioned not far from the Ministry of Defense building at Whitehall, the headquarters of MI6 at Vauxhall, and the home of the Prime Minister at 10 Downing Street. Since the Second World War, the organization has been headquartered in a series of underground tunnels that spread from underneath its central HQ below the Thames. Like most Shadow Agencies, Equinox's existence is known only to those at the highest levels of government. Initially formed to combat the Nazis during World War Two, Equinox's agents have combatted the threat posed by both the Soviet Union and terrorist threats in the years ever since.

One such agent named Nigel Solo had been summoned to the office of Equinox's Director, a man named Felix Proffer, codename: MATCHSTICK. The underground HQ of Equinox was a labyrinthine structure that resembled for the most part at least the interior of an office building. Nigel knocked on the door. After hearing a muffled grunt that sounded like "come in" from the other side, he entered. Seated behind his desk was Felix Proffer himself, an older man with a cold hardened face that had seen and done too much. His hair was gray and he was dressed in a white shirt, gray pants, gray blazer, black tie, and black vest.

Felix's office was adorned with bookcases and a computer screen on the wall behind his desk. "Sit down," he grunted without looking up as he shuffled through papers on his desk.

Obediently, Nigel sat down in one of the chairs in front of Felix's desk. Finally having found the folder he was looking for, Felix slowly looked up from his desk at Nigel.

"I have an assignment for you, Nigel," said Felix bluntly. "It's nothing serious, just an interview."

"An interview, sir?" asked Nigel curiously.

"Yes, MI6 received a request from Interpol regarding Intel on the Devil Woman," answered Felix.

Upon hearing the name, Nigel only grew more and more confused. "Sir, she's dead," he replied stubbornly.

"I know, but apparently Interpol has reason to think the bitch is still among the land of the living," answered Felix.

Nigel was not the kind of man who was prone to being surprised, but this rocked him to his core. He didn't dwell on the past, as in his profession that tended to cost an agent his future, but that name brought back memories that were almost impossible to suppress. Still he maintained his composure.

"Anyway they're sending the man in charge of the investigation over to find out what you know about her, seeing as how you're the only man who ever survived an encounter with her," continued Felix.

"Sir, with all due respect this is ridiculous. We know she's dead. Besides, even if she were still alive she'd have attacked us already," protested Nigel.

"I agree, but either way you're going," said Felix stubbornly.

Suddenly a terrifying possibility crossed Nigel's mind. "Sir, what if she's still alive, then what?" he asked.

Felix Proffer sighed, "If it turns out that she is still alive and this Interpol agent is killed, then we'll know and handle it ourselves."

"So if she is alive then he's bait?" Nigel inquired.

Felix scowled at him, "You can look at it that way but I choose to look at it as outsourcing since I am not going to waste our resources on a wild goose chase… or do you want to tell me how to do my job?"

"No, sir," replied Nigel not wishing to incur the wrath of one of the most dangerous men in the British Government.

"I assume his phone is bugged so we can track him?" asked Nigel.

"Naturally," answered Felix, sounding proud of his cleverness. However if she is still alive the termination order will go to you."

"Thank you, sir," said Nigel, suddenly hoping she was still alive so he could get some payback for all the men who died at her hands, and the torture she put him through.

"Where am I supposed to meet this Interpol agent?" asked Nigel.

"Hyde Park, his name's Barry Mendelsohn, the details are in here," said Felix and he handed Nigel a folder.

Nigel took the folder and opened it. Inside were three pages containing background information on Siobhan and the IRA.

"Give it to him; it contains all the information he needs to know about her, with some obvious redactions of course," said Felix as Nigel skimmed through it.

"Thank you, Sir," replied Nigel expecting nothing more.

"That will be all, you're dismissed," said Felix as he returned to his paperwork.

Nigel Solo nodded and walked out of the office with the folder. On his way to the hidden exit, he tried not to think about how his time was being wasted.

Chapter 4

The Right Direction

Barry Mendelsohn hated flying on commercial airlines because perhaps inevitably on every single flight he was on, there was always a screaming baby making it impossible to sleep or read. Fortunately, the flight from Lyon-Saint-Exupery Airport in Lyon, France to Heathrow in London was only an hour and forty minutes.

After going through security, he walked to the food court and sat down. He checked his phone for any messages and was not surprised to see one there marked Hyde Park from SABRE. The message read: Am waiting in Hyde Park where are you? Mendelsohn typed his response: just arrived in London, then he pressed Send.

He stood up and walked out, glad to be out of the airport at last. Mendelsohn looked around and ran to the first cab he saw, yelling "Taxi!"

The taxi stopped and he got in. Before the driver could ask, where he wanted to go Mendelsohn said "Hyde Park fast."

The driver smiled and they drove off. As they drove, Mendelsohn reviewed what he had read in the folder Lohman had given him on Siobhan. The file mostly contained information on the IRA with most of its Intel on Siobhan limited to her battles with British Special Forces and speculation as to her background. It wasn't much to go on but he knew that his real lead would come from this SABRE.

*****

Agent Nigel Solo, codename: SABRE, sat waiting for him on a bench pretending to read the latest issue of TIME. This was the second time in three months that he had had a meeting with someone in a park. Though this was different, the last time he was meeting an old friend of his from America on orders from his superiors to determine his future intentions. This was about a ghost from his past, a ghost that refused to cease haunting him. Nigel had tried and failed to put his encounter with the Devil Woman out of his mind when he got this assignment.

Upon arriving at Hyde Park, Mendelsohn paid the taxi driver before getting out of the car. He walked into the park casually. It was overcast with a mild chill in the air, which was typical of the weather in London. Mendelsohn was used to cold weather since he had experienced far worse in Canada but that didn't mean he enjoyed it. As Mendelsohn walked through the park he was somewhat frustrated because he had no idea what SABRE looked like, just that he would be sitting on a bench reading a copy of TIME magazine.

Barry Mendelsohn scanned the park and saw a man in a gray suit reading an issue of TIME.

Mendelsohn walked over to the bench and sat next to him.

Solo looked at the man who just sat down next to him and recognized him as the one he was supposed to meet.

"Took your time getting here, Mr. Mendelsohn," said Solo.

Mendelsohn looked at him glad to have finally met his contact.

SABRE possessed a strong soldierly build, and was wearing, a gray blazer, and pants, with white dress shirt and a black tie. His face and demeanor reminded Mendelsohn of one of the actors who played James Bond, but he couldn't think of which one.

"You must be SABRE," replied Mendelsohn.

"The one and only," said Solo as they shook hands. "Now then, since when did Interpol get in the business of hunting the dead?"

Mendelsohn knew what he was getting at. "We aren't usually, but for people like this Devil Woman we make an exception," he answered with a wry smile.

"Alright then, let's be frank: The Devil Woman is dead and you're wasting time with this investigation," said Solo bluntly.

"If that's so, then why is the Heise She Li Triad so hell-bent on finding her," asked Mendelsohn. "And just so we're clear, there are several other assignments I'd prefer to have than chasing some ghost," he added.

"Not ghost, Devil," said Nigel ominously.

"Look I came here to get a lead on her from you guys. So I'd appreciate some help, not sarcasm," said Mendelsohn starting to get annoyed.

Solo's eyes narrowed and his stare suddenly became serious. "Let me make something absolutely clear: if she's alive then you have no idea who you're up against.

Siobhan's a hardcore super terrorist, the kind of assassin you see in movies, deadly with anything you can think of – guns, knives or her bare hands."

"So I keep hearing," Barry replied.

"Hearing and seeing are two very different things, when the IRA wanted someone taken out with extreme prejudice, they called her and she was one hundred percent effective."

"What makes you such an expert?" asked Mendelsohn.

Nigel Solo sighed as he relived the blood soaked memories of long ago. "Years ago, when I was in the SAS, my unit was sent into Northern Ireland to kill her and the other members of her IRA faction, it was the five of us against the three of them, so naturally we thought we had them, as would anyone," said Nigel.

"We were approaching their hideout, then all of a sudden she comes flying out with a goddamn paperclip and kills four of us with the bloody thing, but left me alive to interrogate.

"For two months I was tortured at her hands then left for dead in a bloody shack. By the time a rescue arrived, she was long gone. Two years later she blew herself up," finished Solo.

"Come on, a paperclip? Really?"

"A fucking paperclip," grunted Nigel.

Mendelsohn could tell by the tone of his voice and the look on his face that he was telling the truth as crazy as it sounded.

"Do you know how she got her name?" Solo asked.

"Because of her red hair."

"No, she got it after she firebombed several British government buildings in Dublin."

"What about her motivation?"

"What?" asked Nigel, confused?

"Every terrorist has a motivation: Bin Laden, Kaczynski, and The Jackal. What was hers?"

Nigel shrugged. "I don't know. Hell, only she knows and she's dead."

"Why do you think she's dead?"

"Because we have a body, not to mention the fact that if she were still alive then she would have attacked us again already," answered Nigel.

Barry was quiet for a minute as he absorbed everything that Solo had said. Suddenly a question occurred to him. "What about her three accomplices?"

Solo looked confused for a minute then realized what he meant.

"After she died they split up and we ended up killing two of them and catching one, the captured one's name is Davin Tierney."

"What happened to him?"

Nigel handed him the file Felix had given him. "It's all in here," he answered.

Suddenly Solo's phone started ringing; he picked it up, and saw that there was a message from MATCHSTICK. He quickly returned the phone to his pocket and looked at Mendelsohn.

"Listen I have to go, take this and call if you have any more questions; ask for SABRE," said Solo and handed Mendelsohn a card with a phone number on it before standing up.

Mendelsohn stood up too and both men shook hands.

"One more thing before I go, Mr. Mendelsohn," said Solo as that serious look on his face had returned. "If she is alive and you find her, do not hesitate to pull the trigger as many times as you can because if you do hesitate, you'll be dead before you hit the floor," finished Solo.

"Noted," said Barry Mendelsohn as they walked out of the park.

Having left Mendelsohn, Nigel Solo walked to his car on the other side of the park, a black Aston Martin Vanquish that had been given several enhancements by Equinox's technicians. Meanwhile Mendelsohn tried to find a taxi that would take him to the Interpol building in London.

However, both of them were unaware that their entire conversation was being secretly recorded by agents of two separate clandestine organizations, who were now heading back to their respective offices to send this information to their superiors. Both of these agents were unaware of each other's presence in Hyde Park.

One of them was Chinese and a member of the Chinese Heise She Li Triad. He calmly walked to his car and began to drive back to the Triads hidden London office to relay what he had learned to the man in charge of the Triads hunt for Siobhan Costello.

The other man was a native of Wales and a member of a secret organization known as the Order of the Silent Disciples that was also searching for Siobhan Costello. He made his way to a car waiting to take him back to the Apostolic Nunciature, which served as Vatican Cities embassy to the United Kingdom. Once he was there, he would send

what he had just learned to his superiors in
Vatican City.

*****

Upon returning to his car, Nigel pulled out his
phone and dialed MATCHSTICK's number.

After a few rings, he was greeted by Felix
Proffer's voice.

"You called Sir," said Nigel.

"Yes, sorry to interrupt you but we have a
problem and this is urgent."

"What is it sir?"

"We've been monitoring your
conversation with Mendelsohn and we
discovered that someone else was also
listening in on it," answered MATCHSTICK.

"Who?"

"We don't know yet but we're waiting for
them to make their next move so stand by for
further orders," said MATCHSTICK. "Do you
have your pistol with you?"

"One moment, sir," said Nigel as he
lowered the phone and leaned over to the
glove compartment. He opened the
compartment and placed his thumb on a
hidden thumbprint scanner. In response, a
hidden tray slid out containing his weapon of

choice: A 7.62 millimeter Walther PPK with two magazines and a silencer next to it. He leaned away from it and raised the phone back to his ear.

"Yes sir," he answered.

"Good, you will need it later once we find out who has been listening in on your conversation," replied MATCHSTICK.

"Sir, do you think that this verifies whether Siobhan is still alive?" asked Nigel.

MATCHSTICK was silent for a minute. Then he said, "I don't know, though it does lend some credence to it." He added, "It is clear to me now that we aren't the only ones interested in the Devil Woman. Standby for further orders," he said before hanging up.

Nigel Solo returned the phone to his pocket; he looked at the Walther and leaned over to pick up the gun, the silencer and one magazine. He placed the magazine and silencer on the seat next to him and put the gun in his other hand. He had a feeling that this mission would require considerable subtlety so he screwed the silencer onto the barrel of the pistol. Finally, he picked up the magazine and slid it into the gun.

He switched on the safety and placed the gun back in the tray.

Satisfied, Nigel then gently pushed the tray back into the compartment and closed the glove compartment door. His mission accomplished, he decided to wait for MATCHSTICK's call at a nearby pub known as the Dog and Bull.

*****

Barry Mendelsohn checked into a small hotel not far from Interpol's office in London. The room was small and consisted of a bed, TV and a desk with a chair by the window. He placed his suitcase next to the bed tossed the folder on the bed then he removed his coat and placed it on the back of the chair. He didn't bother to open his case, as he knew he would only be there for a few hours. He loosened his tie, picked up the folder and sat down on the bed deciding to read the folder. The picture of her in this one was just as grainy as the one Lohman showed him and the first page contained the same information so he skipped to the second one.

It began:

The IRA was formed and led by Davin Tierney (see next page for members) a high-ranking member of the Provisional Irish Republican Army (PIRA). Its membership consisted of Davin Tierney, Siobhan Costello, Mara O Guinn, and Seamus Kennedy. It is unknown how Tierney recruited Siobhan who served as the IRA's chief enforcer and assassin. Similar to the PIRA the IRA's stated goal is Ireland's unification and liberation from what they see as British control; however, they also sought to wipe out and destroy England by waging war and terrorist attacks. It is this ultranationalist ideology and subsequent terrorist actions that led to them being condemned by the IRA's current leadership. Tierney has promised to kill a hundred British people for every year Ireland has been under British control. He has also promised to personally execute the IRA leaders that signed the Good Friday Agreement in 1998 believing them to be traitors to the cause of a free and united Ireland.

Sounds like the Irish version of ISIS, thought Barry. He looked at the pictures of them on the bottom of the page. Davin was a rough looking white-haired man with an unsettling grin on his face. The same picture of Siobhan was next to him, and next to her was a picture of Mara O'Guinn, a woman with spiky raven hair and freckles on her face and a crazy grin while Seamus Kennedy was a large, bald brute of a man. Since they were both dead, he skipped the information on them deciding to read it later and focusing on Siobhan and the only other surviving member of their cell, Davin Tierney. He studied the picture of Tierney; he was a rough looking man with combed white hair and eyes that reeked of madness, the eyes of a fanatic but also a tactician.

Davin Tierney, born in Dublin Ireland, to an unknown Irish Prostitute and an abusive father, Lance Tierney who fought with IRA forces during the Troubles from 1975 to 1988. In 1990, his father was arrested and was sent to HM Prison Maze for being complicit in an attempted bombing where he ultimately died in a prison riot. Since his mother was deemed unfit to take care of him, the five-year-old Davin was placed in the care of his elderly grandfather, an extreme Irish nationalist, who instilled in him a strong hatred of the British and a sense of loyalty to the IRA's cause. Following the signing of the 1998 Good Friday agreement, Davin, and his uncle left Ireland along with several other IRA loyalists and went to Libya where Davin underwent military training for two years. During this time his grandfather died of old age. In 2000, Davin returned to Ireland and briefly rejoined the IRA but was soon expelled due to his violent nature and agenda.

Deciding to wage a war against the British government himself, he spent the next five years searching for possible recruits. During this time, he came into contact with Seamus Kennedy, Mara O'Guinn and Siobhan Costello. Having assembled his team he spent the next five years training them in guerilla tactics and intelligence gathering. Upon completing their training, they began calling themselves The IRA.

Over the next several years, Tierney masterminded a campaign of terrorist attacks and robberies all over the United Kingdom. It is also believed that while in Libya he made contact with {REDACTED}.

Barry rolled his eyes upon seeing the word though he couldn't help but wonder what was redacted as he kept reading.

Who it is believed provided him with support. We also believe he has made contact with several underworld figures such as the Guild assassin: Katyusha and the thief known as the Smiling Fox.

The Smiling Fox? Thought Barry surprised.

It is unknown whether or not he knows the true identity of the Smiling Fox.

Following Siobhan Costello's death, the IRA split up, and Davin was caught in an SAS raid led by and after standing trial

Tierney was sentenced to life in prison. He is currently serving his sentence.

By the time he was done, it was starting to get dark; he was tired and began to yawn. Barry decided to read the rest later before heading up to Wakefield.

Chapter 5

A Hundred Miles from Nowhere

The nightmare was always the same; it was night and Siobhan was in the back seat of the car driving with a remote control. In the trunk was a block of C4 and in the front passenger seat was a corpse that matched her appearance and blood type. The car was driving towards the royal family's vacation home, Balmoral Castle.

When she was close, she would roll down the window and yell out the motto of the IRA. "Our day will come!" which would bring the castle guards running.

Then just before the shooting started, she would jump out of the car. When the car was close, enough she pressed the detonator causing it to explode several feet from the gates. She ran away from the castle satisfied with the success of her plan. However, it was at this point in the nightmare that the ghosts of her many victims appeared, they swarmed out of nowhere looking like smoke with hate in their black pits of eyes. They pointed at her as they moaned the word "Guilty" over and over again.

She had tried pleading for their forgiveness to no avail. As she looked into their eyes she could see them dying by her hand. Then in the midst of the phantasm's recriminations, the ground would suddenly crack open and she would fall into a pit of fire as the surrounding ghosts cheered at her damnation.

"No!" yelled Siobhan as she woke up and sat up in bed, her body covered in a cold sweat.

She looked around relieved to be surrounded by the familiar environment of her room. Ever since she came to the Convent Siobhan's nights were plagued by the dream. Is that a sign of what awaits me for my sins? She wondered as she wiped the sweat from her brow. She buried her face in her hands mentally exhausted by the dream. Are these dreams a premonition of what awaits me in hell, she thought with a shudder. She lifted her head out of her hands and looked out the window of her tiny room to see the sun shining and to hear the birds chirping in the morning. She smiled, relieved at the comforting site outside the window.

Then she looked under the bed and her smile faded as her trunk was still there — locked as always. The trunk and the tattoo on her back were the only reminders of a murderous past that Siobhan regretted every second of her life. She got out of bed, walked to her dresser and looked at her body in the mirror; her underwear and bra were soaked in cold sweat. She often wondered if Sisters Luna and Garcia were intimidated by her height and muscle. She shrugged as she brushed such thoughts aside and put on a clean bra and underwear, plain white T-shirt, gray pants and the nuns habit.

She walked out of her room and down the hallway toward the dining room where they would all meet and have breakfast. As she approached the room, she could hear the sound of a TV. She opened the door of the dining room and found Sister Luna, Sister Garcia and Mother Lucrezia sitting at the table. They were intently watching a news program on the television. Siobhan was about to say good morning when Mother Lucrezia turned to face her and put her finger to her lips and said "Shhh" then turned back to face the television.

Curiously, Siobhan walked over to the table, sat down, and watched the TV just as the news program cut to a commercial. Luna and Garcia looked at each other nervously while Mother Lucrezia dipped her spoon in her cereal, her face impassive as usual.

"What is it?" asked Siobhan the three of them looked at her surprised at her question.

"A rogue FARC militia is moving towards Malvara," Mother Lucrezia explained calmly as she continued to eat her cereal.

Siobhan instantly understood why they were nervous because she was well aware of how brutally violent the FARC was, as she had visited a FARC camp when she was in the IRA. They were as fanatical as her compatriots in the IRA. She also knew that they received weaponry and equipment from Cuba and Venezuela but she didn't know if this was still the case.

"They're saying they intend to take over the town and use it as a base," said Sister Luna.

"When will they be here?" Siobhan asked.

"The news said late tomorrow," answered Sister Luna.

"Maybe we should leave like they said," Sister Garcia supposed. Siobhan was wondering about that too.

"Nonsense," said Mother Lucrezia.

They all looked at her quizzically. "But Mother Lucrezia, what about FARC? If they get here they'll kill us," said Sister Luna.

"Do you know what they do to women?" joined in Sister Garcia.

Siobhan could hear the fear in the young girls' voices. They were ignorant of the world of blood and death that Siobhan had wasted her life in for so long. She could not defend them against such danger.

Mother Lucrezia looked up from her bowl of cereal. "Have you forgotten Psalm 23:4, young ones?"

Sister Garcia and Luna looked at each other confused at the question.

"Even though I walk through the valley of the shadow of death, I will fear no evil, for you are with me; your rod and your staff, they comfort me," said Mother Lucrezia calmly. "God will protect us from these evil men, now finish your cereal we have to go to the shelter and cook dinner for the unfortunates," she finished.

Must be Tuesday thought Siobhan.

The two girls nodded obediently and finished eating while Siobhan readied her breakfast though she could still see the fear in their eyes. When they were done eating, they put their cereal bowls in the sink to clean later. With their breakfast finished, they all left the convent for the shelter.

As they walked through the town, the townspeople looked nervous. There were several cars driving out of the town, loaded with their belongings.

"I guess they heard the news," said Siobhan.

Mother Lucrezia ignored them while Garcia and Luna couldn't help but feel nervous. Siobhan looked at them comfortingly as they walked to the shelter.

"Don't worry, Mother Lucrezia was right. God will protect us," said Siobhan smiling warmly.

They seemed relieved at her words. "Thank you Sister Darcy," said Sister Luna.

"By the way Sister Darcy I heard you screaming earlier are you okay" she asked.

"Don't worry about it, it was just a bad dream," said Siobhan dismissively.

Upon arriving at the shelter, they began to prepare the kitchen. "What are we serving today?" asked Sister Garcia.

"Tomato soup," answered Mother Lucrezia bluntly.

"Again?" muttered Sister Garcia.

"What's wrong with my tomato soup," asked Mother Lucrezia.

"Nothing," said Sister Garcia defensively with a sheepish smile.

"Smooth," whispered Sister Luna dryly to Sister Garcia.

Siobhan smiled silently at the humorous exchange between the two as she began to prepare the food.

Chapter 6

Word on the Street

There is a region of the Philippine Sea known as the Devils Sea, where ships and planes have disappeared for centuries. However, within the Sea is a small landmass known as Sankan Island; it is referred to, among other things, as the capital city of the underworld. The reason for this unique sobriquet is because the island is controlled by two of the world's largest criminal organizations: The Chinese Heise She Li Triad, and the Russian mafia known as the Vasilev Syndicate.

The small city on the island was dominated by two massive skyscrapers. One of them was the regional office of the Triad while the other served as the regional office of the Syndicate.

The man who oversaw the Triads operations on the island was known as Deng. At the moment, he was gazing out at his kingdom from his office on the top floor of the Triads building. He looked out at the city below him like a medieval king surveying his lands. However, his thoughts were elsewhere, he had been reflecting on the events of the last three months in an effort to gain a new perspective on the mission the Mountain Master had given him. It had been three months since the Triad and their allies in the Vasilev Syndicate had forced the Rojas cartel off the island, and since he had met Simon Kane, the former CIA agent who had rescued the Mountain Master's daughter from the cartel during the conflict.

Now the island had returned to what passed for normal and the territory previously controlled by the cartel had been divided between the Triad and the Russian Vasilev Syndicate. At the conclusion of the conflict with the cartel, the Mountain Master, in return for Simon's rescue of his daughter, promised to assist Kane in destroying their mutual enemy: The Networc by assembling a team for him.

The Mountain Master had given Deng a list of two people to find for this team and put him in charge of the search. The first name on the list was a guild assassin codenamed: MAGIC 44. He had done work for the Triad before and was the easier of the two to find, so Deng decided to contact him last. The second name on the list, and the subject of Deng's current headache, was Siobhan Costello. Over the last three months, he had deployed agents all over the world to find her. Yet despite the full resources of the Triad at his disposal, they had come up with nothing.

It was frustrating because Deng had been given six months to find her and MAGIC 44. He briefly entertained the idea of contacting Kane for assistance but the last he checked, Kane was somewhere in the Middle East acting as a bodyguard for the Mountain Master's daughter thus making Kane unavailable anyway. Just then, a knock on the door interrupted his reflection.

Deng sighed, "so much for a new perspective," he muttered as he turned to his desk.

He sat down and looked at the small console next to his computer monitor. On the console was a small screen with two buttons. In front of it, the screen showed who was at the door, while the buttons controlled the door's electronic locks. The screen showed that the man at the door was Mazin Ho, Deng's second in command; in his left hand, he had a folder.

Deng pushed a button on the console and the door opened. Mazin walked in, a faint hint of a smile on his face.

"You look pleased," said Deng dryly as he leaned back in his chair lazily.

"With good reason you see, I have good news," answered Mazin as he approached the desk.

"Well? Go on. The suspense is killing me," said Deng sarcastically as Mazin sat down in one of the two chairs in front of the desk.

"Several hours ago one of our guys in London was conducting surveillance on a meeting between an MI6 agent and an

Interpol agent," said Mazin as he handed Deng the folder.

Deng opened it and pulled out a photograph of two men on a bench.

"We've identified the man on the right as an MI6 agent named Nigel Solo, and the man on the left is an Interpol agent named Barry Mendelsohn," said Mazin as Deng studied the picture.

Deng placed them on the desk. "So?"

"You see, according to the conversation our London office recorded between these two," said Mazin as he pointed to Mendelsohn in the picture. "This man has been tasked by Interpol to track down and capture Siobhan Costello and he was interviewing this British spy for any possible leads." He continued, "According to Solo, there's an inmate at Wakefield Prison called Davin Tierney that used to fight alongside her in the IRA."

Deng listened intently.

"We believe Mendelsohn is going there to interview him," Mazin added.

Deng thought for a minute analyzing everything Mazin had said; then an ingenious idea came to him. "Do we have anyone in that prison?" asked Deng.

"Yes, want me to contact them and have them interrogate Tierney?"

"No" replied Deng.

Mazin was surprised by the answer. "Why?" he inquired.

"Because, it is important that we not tip our hand since we don't know who else might be looking for her, instead let Interpol find her for us," answered Deng.

"Forgive me, but I don't understand," replied Mazin.

"Have all available resources place Mendelsohn under surveillance and he'll lead us to her, if she's even alive in the first place, and once he finds her and brings her out into the open we make our move and send a team to make contact with her," explained Deng.

"A risky stratagem, sir, but wouldn't it be easier to hire the Flying Fish Trading Company to get her?"

"In some ways yes, but I don't want to be seen as relying on them too much, remember with the Rojas Cartel gone, it's just us and the Vasilev Syndicate on the island now," replied

Deng. "And even we must play the game of politics,"

"I see. I'll contact our overseas branches," replied Mazin.

"Good, notify me immediately if there's any changes," Deng ordered.

"Of course, sir," said Mazin as he stood up and walked out of the office.

Once he was gone, Deng turned and looked out the window. "Where are you little Devil?" he muttered.

*****

Thousands of miles away in Vatican City not far from St Peters Basilica sat an unassuming office building. Unknown to all who passed it, except for the pope himself, the building was in actuality the headquarters of the most secret organization in Vatican City, the elite black ops intelligence agency known as the Order of the Silent Disciples, commonly referred to by its members as Disciple 13. Their primary task is to assassinate elements threatening the church as well as gather intelligence on foreign powers and organizations. Their leader is chosen by his Holiness himself. Its current leader was a

Bishop named Marzano; he was an Italian man in his late fifties with the wrinkled face of someone who had seen too much.

At the moment, he was sitting in his office working on his computer when he heard a knock on the door. He looked up and pushed a button on his desk causing the doors to swing open. Into the office walked one of the Order's intelligence analysts, a young man named Reno.

"What is it, Reno? I'm very busy," said Bishop Marzano.

"Sir, our agent in London was eavesdropping on a meeting between an Equinox agent and an Interpol agent in Hyde park several hours ago."

Marzano sighed and leaned back in his chair; for multiple reasons the Order of the Silent Disciples has never been on good terms with MI6, specifically their shadowy division known as Equinox.

"So what did he find out?" asked Marzano.

"The Interpol agent was interviewing the other man about the Devil Woman.

Apparently they think she's still alive and he's searching for her," answered Reno.

Marzano was a hard man to surprise, but upon hearing this news, he was quite surprised. He had read a great deal about this woman since Disciple 13 had given her IRA faction support. He remembered field reports from his agents calling her a devout Catholic and a highly efficient soldier among other things.

"What do we do about this, sir?" asked Reno curiously.

"Let me think, Reno," replied Marzano.

If there was even a chance that she was still alive, she could possibly be recruited and would make a huge asset, thought Marzano.

He looked up at Reno, having made up his mind. "Reno, I want you to notify our foreign operatives to track the progress of this Interpol agent and notify us immediately, understood?" ordered Marzano.

"Yes, sir," said Reno and nodded. "But sir, I'm curious why bother?" he asked.

"Because Reno, if this Devil Woman is still alive she may prove useful to us, now go."

"Yes sir," said Reno with a nod; he walked out of the office and closed the door behind him.

*****

Located not far from Hyde Park, the Dog and Bull served as the preferred watering hole for various Equinox agents. It was an upscale pub visited by the more upper class members of British society. However, neither its owner nor employees and patrons were aware that many of the customers were spies. At the moment the bar was mostly empty, Nigel was seated in a leather chair drinking a vodka tonic and reading the latest edition of the Daily Telegraph. The cover story focused on the plight of Belarusian refugees fleeing the country and the strain it placed on the already fractured European Union. Suddenly Nigel's phone rang; he lowered the newspaper and retrieved his phone from his pocket. He saw that the call was from MATCHSTICK, he raised the phone to his ear.

"Yes, sir," said Nigel.

"We've managed to pinpoint where the listener is," said MATCHSTICK. "The listener is based out of a Chinese restaurant called the

Velvet Dragon, which according to Scotland Yard and MI5 is a front for the Triad.

"I'm sending you the address now and a picture of the target, so take care of it," said MATCHSTICK before hanging up.

Nigel lowered the phone and saw a text from MATCHSTICK that had a picture of a surly looking Chinese man with the restaurants address below it. Nigel shrugged annoyed that he had to drive across the city to get there. Casually, he tossed the paper on the wooden coffee table in front of him. He stood up, straightened his tie, and exited the pub.

Chapter 7

Off With a Bang

Nigel Solo parked across the street from the Velvet Dragon. He glanced out the window at the restaurant; it looked like a stereotypical Chinese Restaurant with two floors. Nigel opened the glove compartment, placed his thumb on the scanner and the tray with his Walther slid out. He picked up the gun and attached the suppressor to the barrel.

He put one of the two magazines in the gun and slid the other in his coat pocket. Nigel switched off the safety and finally slid the gun into the shoulder holster under his blazer. He looked up at the sky; the typical gray London sky was slowly being replaced by the darker skies of the night. Nigel had committed the picture of his target to memory. He was about to get out of the car when he noticed a rough looking Chinese man walk into the alley next to the restaurant.

Nigel waited till he was gone then he got out of the car. Casually he walked across the street and into the alley. Upon entering the alley Nigel started walking much slower so as not to attract any attention. As he walked down the alley, he heard men speaking in Mandarin at the end of the alley. Instinctively, he placed his hand on the butt of his Walther, ready to draw it. As he got closer, he could hear them talking more clearly.

It is standard protocol that all Equinox agents be proficient in various languages. Nigel, who spoke Mandarin, listened to the men speaking carefully. "Do you have it," said one of the men in Mandarin.

Nigel gingerly peeked around the corner and saw a small clearing with metal stairs leading to a back door on the second floor of the restaurant. In the middle of the clearing was the man he saw enter the alley speaking with his target. His target was holding a packet of what looked like it could be cocaine.

Nigel leaned back behind his cover; he drew his Walther and took a deep breath visualizing where they were. Suddenly Nigel leaned out from cover and fired one bullet at the forehead of his target, then he quickly changed targets and fired another shot at the back of the head of the other man. Both his targets' bodies hit the floor, the silencer reducing the gunshots to a barely audible whisper. Slowly, his gun still drawn, Nigel walked towards their bodies. Convinced they were dead Nigel walked up the stairs to the back door. Fortunately, the door was not locked; Nigel opened it carefully and saw a man sitting at a computer, his back to him.

Nigel ran up behind him, grabbed him by the back of his neck, and smashed his face into the computer screen. The man was out cold and his face covered in blood and broken glass. Nigel tossed him to the floor and looked around the desk. It was a cluttered space filled with office supplies and papers. However, on the far side of the desk was a digital camera.

Nigel picked it up and started scanning through the pictures until he saw a picture of himself and Barry talking at Hyde Park.

"Bloody hell," muttered Nigel as he put the camera in his pocket. He also noticed several sim cards and flash drives on the desk next to the computer. Nigel picked them up and put them in his pants pocket. He turned and saw that the man was still out cold.

"If you wanted my picture just ask," said Nigel sardonically as he walked out of the office.

Nigel quickly descended the stairs and returned his Walther to his shoulder holster as he walked back through the alley. He crossed the street and got back in his car. He pulled out his cellphone and dialed MATCHSTICK's number. After a few rings, he was greeted by MATCHSTICK's electronically scrambled voice.

"It's taken care of, Sir; the Triad's definitely interested in the Devil Woman, according to what I've found," said Nigel.

"Excellent work, SABRE. I'll send a cleanup crew. As for you, return to HQ immediately," said MATCHSTICK before hanging up.

*****

Despite the panic caused by the encroaching FARC militia, those who were still in Malvara slept peacefully in their beds that night. In the convent on the far side of town, the four nuns were also asleep after having spent the day and evening preparing food at the homeless shelter. Suddenly a loud explosion in the distance woke them. They quickly got dressed and ran to the windows at the front of the convent to see what caused the explosion. They all met in the lobby of the convent and looked out the window in horror.

In the distance, they could see fire and smoke rising from Malvara.

The air was thick with the echoes of machine gun fire and screaming. Though she said nothing, Siobhan could tell instantly that the guns were AK-47s, the standard issue firearm of the FARC. Suddenly a ball of light shot up from the ground and hit the steeple on the town hall building. A loud fiery explosion sent the steeple to the ground.

Siobhan recognized it as RPG fire. Sister Garcia and Sister Luna turned away from the window, shaken from what they saw, their faces covered in fear. Mother Lucrezia continued looking through the window, her face blank and emotionless as usual. Siobhan wondered how she could be this calm and impassive in the face of such danger. Finally, Mother Lucrezia closed the curtains, and then turned to face her fellow sisters. The room was quiet and then Sister Garcia spoke.

"We should leave now," she said meekly. Siobhan agreed with her but decided to say nothing.

"She's right," replied Sister Luna.

"They control the roads and if we left, where would we go?" asked Mother Lucrezia. Garcia and Luna knew she was right.

"So what do we do?" asked Siobhan.

"For now let's go to bed and tomorrow we shall talk more about this," said Lucrezia.

Luna and Garcia nodded feeling reassured; Siobhan couldn't help but feel nervous. As they, walked back to their rooms Siobhan put her arm around the nervous Sister Garcia and smiled warmly.

"It'll be all right, Sister Garcia. God will protect us," said Siobhan comfortingly.

Sister Garcia smiled, "thank you, Sister Darcy."

Once she was back in her room, Siobhan realized she couldn't sleep since her mind was racing trying out figure out what to do. She sat on the edge of her bed and put her head in her hands as more sounds of terror and pain rang out from the town behind her. Suddenly in the midst of her insomnia, an idea occurred to her.

Since I'm far more skilled at combat than those that were conscripted by the FARC, then perhaps I should attack them covertly, thought Siobhan, remembering the locked trunk under her bed she brought with her from Ireland.

"No," she muttered quickly discarding the idea as she reminded herself of the vow she made to never kill again. Besides she realized it would probably bring with it violent reprisals against the others. She wrestled with the idea. She knew the kind of people rampaging through Malvara. They were all too familiar to Siobhan. These men were violent killers that represented the kind of pointless ideological pursuit that drove her to leave the IRA three years ago.

When she looked out the window at the embattled city beyond her window, she was reminded of all the people she killed and all the friends. She lost in an endless bloody contest that was old when her parents were young. Were these men sent here by God to punish me for my sins she asked? If so, then why did so many innocents have to die? Even I've repented and forsaken violence, so was this part of some test by the Lord, she wondered before finally falling asleep. That morning, for the first time in years, she didn't go out for her exercise and slept instead, not wanting to risk a confrontation with the FARC forces.

*****

When she woke, she rose from her bed, got dressed in her habit and walked to the dining room to join the others for breakfast. As she walked to the dining room she felt strange not having gone for her morning run. Sister Garcia, Sister Luna, and Mother Lucrezia were sitting at the table eating cereal.

"Any news?" asked Siobhan as she poured herself a bowl of cereal and sat down.

"Nothing, they cut off all communication, we're all alone," said Sister Garcia despondently.

"We should have left when we had the chance," said Sister Luna fatalistically.

"You may leave if you wish," said Mother Lucrezia.

They all looked at her equally surprised and confused.

"I'm serious, it is too dangerous for you to be here, and I have no right to keep you here, so if you wish to leave then you may go," continued Lucrezia.

"What about you?" asked Siobhan her voice tinged with concern and her question echoing what they were all thinking?

"Don't worry about me. I'm staying, I refuse to let those butchers destroy this convent," said Mother Lucrezia.

Just like that, Siobhan had made her decision. She was going to stay. She didn't want Sister Luna, Sister Garcia, and Mother Lucrezia to be here alone. "Then I'm staying as well," she said.

"I'll stay," said Sister Garcia.

"And so will I," said Sister Luna.

Before they could say, another word there was a loud explosion that shook the building.

"What was that?" yelled Sister Garcia; they walked to the lobby in the front of the building to see what had caused it.

As they looked out the windows, they saw to their horror a jeep with the logo of the FARC on it. One of the four men in the jeep stepped out; he was a large burly man dressed entirely in military camouflage and was carrying a bullhorn in his hand. His appearance reminded Siobhan of a comrade she knew from the IRA named Davin.

He raised the bullhorn to his mouth and began to speak. "Attention, we are the Revolutionary Armed Forces of Colombia. We have claimed this town as a garrison and demand that you leave this convent so we can construct a lookout post here," said the man.

Before any of them could say anything, Mother Lucrezia opened the window and yelled, "We will never leave!" at them, then slammed the window shut.

Siobhan and the others were taken aback by this act of defiance from a woman who had never raised her voice. Some of the men in the jeep chuckled smugly at Mother Lucrezia's act of defiance.

"You have two weeks to change your mind otherwise you will suffer the consequences," said the man. He lowered the bullhorn and got in the jeep and they drove off.

Meanwhile in the convent, Sister Luna and Sister Garcia looked at each other nervously. Siobhan remembered her idea from last night and wondered if she was making the right decision.

Chapter 8

Interview in the Monster Mansion

After an almost four-hour drive, Barry Mendelsohn arrived at Wakefield prison. It was a Category A prison, in West Yorkshire, England, reserved for serious offenders like the man Mendelsohn had come here to interview. He had spent the better part of the day before trying to get clearance at HMPS headquarters at Clive House in London to see the man. As he pulled up to the prison, he saw a large man in a suit standing at the front door of the prison.

Mendelsohn stepped out of the rented car and walked over to the man.

"Welcome to Wakefield, Agent Mendelsohn. I'm Warden Hammersmith," said the man as they shook hands.

"My pleasure, Warden, I take it you know why I'm here," said Mendelsohn.

"Yes, they told me you were coming to see Tierney," answered the Warden.

"Shall we?" said Mendelsohn gesturing to the door.

"Of course, follow me," said the Warden as he walked to the door with Mendelsohn.

After surrendering his pistol to the guards, he followed the warden through the prison. They stopped at an elevator and stepped in. "What floor?" asked Mendelsohn curiously.

"I'll get the key," responded Hammersmith and proceeded to remove a small silver necklace from around his neck with a small key on the end.

The warden then opened a small panel on the elevator wall and revealing a small key hole. The warden placed the key in the hole and twisted it to the left. The elevator began to move downward. It began to dawn on Mendelsohn that this was no ordinary prison.

The warden looked at him as if he could tell what he was thinking.

"I bet you have some questions," said the Warden.

"A few, is this some kind of black site?" Mendelsohn asked.

The Warden shrugged.

Before Mendelsohn could utter a reply, the elevator stopped and the doors opened. They were staring down a white hallway with a steel door at the end of it.

"Right this way, Mr. Mendelsohn," said the Warden as he stepped out of the elevator toward the door.

Mendelsohn followed him, but as he walked through the hallway, he could tell he was being watched. The Warden opened the door, which led to another hallway, only this one had doors on the walls with roman numerals on them. At the end of the hallway was a steel door with the words: Conference Room written on it.

"I have a dumb question: are those cells?" asked Mendelsohn gesturing to the doors on his right and left.

"Yes, and that is a dumb question," answered the Warden. "He's in here, behind bulletproof glass," said the warden before opening the door. Mendelsohn walked into the room as the door closed behind him. The room was of medium size with a glass partition dividing it in half. On Mendelsohn's side of the room was a small chair. He walked to the chair and sat down. On the other side of the glass partition sitting in a chair was Davin Tierney.

His hands were handcuffed under the chair, which was bolted to the floor. He was wearing an orange prison jumpsuit. He was a thin looking man, with a tired diamond shaped face and short unkempt white hair. Mendelsohn was struck by his black eyes; there was an unhinged wildness in them. They reminded Mendelsohn of the eyes of mass shooters, utterly devoid of sanity and with a desire to see the world burn.

"Good afternoon, Mr. Tierney, I have some questions for you," said Mendelsohn calmly.

"I don't talk to goddamn Englishmen," replied Tierney angrily.

Mendelsohn sighed impatiently; he could tell right from the start that Tierney was going to make this difficult.

"I'm actually Canadian," replied Mendelsohn dryly.

"There a difference?" grunted Tierney, grinning at his cleverness.

Mendelsohn ignored the comment. "Mr. Tierney, I am not interested in you or what you've done; I'm actually more concerned with a late associate of yours: Siobhan Costello," said Mendelsohn plainly.

At the mention of the name, a look of both pride and confusion appeared on Tierney's face. "Haven't you heard the Devil Woman is dead?" he asked rhetorically.

Despite his bluster, Mendelsohn could tell that he had some doubt about her status. "Mr. Tierney, I have heard a great many things about her recently and it seems to me that someone with her skills and training could fake her death successfully, right?" said Mendelsohn.

"She was the best of the best," Tierney replied.

"So I'm told, now hypothetically speaking…" began Mendelssohn.

"I didn't know Interpol dealt in hypotheticals," interrupted Tierney.

"When we have to," replied Barry dismissively.

"Now, if she did fake her death, she would obviously leave the country and with her skills that is easily done," said Mendelsohn. "And according to our files, you and she traveled to a number of countries for various reasons, countries where it would be easy, even for someone like her to disappear. So, if she were still alive, what country would she go to?" asked Mendelsohn.

Tierney thought for a minute, Mendelsohn guessed he was weighing his options. After a few minutes, Tierney looked directly at Mendelsohn, grinning wickedly. "Malvara, he said smiling smugly at Mendelsohn.

Mendelsohn was confused. "Never heard of it," he said.

"It's a small town in the middle of the Colombian jungle, great place to disappear," answered Tierney.

"Why would she go there?"

"Years ago we drove through the town on the way to buy some guns from some FARC guys and she was really taken with the place," said Tierney. "She had a look on her face like she had found paradise or something. You don't see shit like the rainforest growing up in Ireland, he added."

"Thank you, by the way why is she called the Devil Woman?" asked Mendelsohn.

Davin smiled, "Because she sends Englishman to hell where they belong."

Mendelsohn stood up to leave, he was positive that he had extracted every bit of information that he could from Tierney. As he walked to the door, he heard Tierney mumble something.

Mendelsohn turned around to face him. "What?" he asked.

"I said you'll never find her," barked Tierney.

"And if I do?" asked Mendelsohn.

"Then you'll join the Brits in hell and I'll be sitting here laughing at your stupidity," said Tierney confidently.

"Again, I'm Canadian," said Mendelsohn as he knocked on the door.

A few seconds later, it opened and Mendelsohn walked out of the room only to be greeted by Warden Hammersmith.

"Well how'd it go?" asked the Warden.

"Good, I think," replied Mendelsohn.

Mendelsohn followed the warden back to the elevator and out of the prison.

All the while Tierney's words reverberated throughout Mendelsohn's mind. Once he was in his car, Mendelsohn got out his cellphone and sent a message to the Director of Interpol in Bogota, Colombia, Manuel Gaspar. The message contained the details of his mission—to look into Malvara, since he had to go there. He checked the times for the next available flight to Colombia and to his dismay; he saw it was the following day. He added his arrival date, and then clicked send.

"Figures," muttered Mendelsohn as he returned the phone to his pocket. He drove to the nearest hotel for some needed rest. He was unaware that at that moment in Vatican City, London and Sankan his message had been intercepted and was being read by Disciple 13 and the Heise She Li Triad.

Chapter 9

The Short Straw

For the next two days, the nuns stayed in the convent, too nervous to venture into the town. To keep their minds distracted the four of them spent their time cleaning and reading. Often Siobhan would pray to God asking for help, sometimes joined by her fellow sisters. Occasionally Siobhan would think about attacking the guerillas and each time she brushed it aside remembering her vow. However, on the morning of the third day, they discovered they were out of food.

They sat at the table in the kitchen staring at each other. They all knew what they had to do and what could happen if they went into Malvara to get food. Siobhan and Mother

Lucrezia did not show it, but they were both nervous.

"Let's draw straws, shortest straw goes," Mother Lucrezia suggested.

The three of them nodded in agreement, Mother Lucrezia walked to the pantry and got four straws of various lengths then sat back down.

As the four of them drew straws Siobhan prayed to herself that she would get the short straw thus sparing the others from any harm, if only temporarily. Once the straws were drawn, they compared the sizes. To Siobhan's horror, she found that her straw was the tallest. She looked around the table to see who had the short straw.

"I guess it's me," said Sister Garcia putting on a brave face. But Siobhan could tell she was terrified.

They were silent for a minute. I'm ready to die but she has her whole life ahead of her, thought Siobhan. Sister Garcia stood up and looked at them.

"I guess I had better get going, while it's still light out," said Sister Garcia with a brave smile trying to sound as strong as she could.

They nodded solemnly in response, too frightened and too nervous to say anything.

Sister Garcia walked over to the counter and grabbed their shopping list for the market. They followed her to the front door and said a prayer for her to be safe, followed by a hug.

Sister Garcia walked out of the convent and down the dirt road into town. Through the window, Siobhan watched her and she asked herself why Sister Garcia had to pick the short straw.

For hours, they waited for Sister Garcia to return, doing whatever they could to keep themselves from worrying about her. Mother Lucrezia and Sister Luna were reading in the small library at the back of the convent.

Siobhan sat at the altar on her knees and prayed. "My Lord what should I do? Deliver us from this evil. Please give me an answer," she prayed under her breath.

As if in answer, something slammed in to the front door of the convent followed by a barely audible whine. Mother Lucrezia and Sister Luna ran to the front of the convent upon hearing the noise.

"What was that?" asked Sister Luna, the three of them walked to the door and opened it cautiously. In front of the convent was a jeep with three FARC guerillas snickering at something on the stairs.

The nuns shifted there gaze to the stairs only to see the unconscious, beaten and scarred body of Sister Garcia. Her face was bloody and swollen and her clothes were in tatters. Before the nuns could react, the guerillas started the jeep and drove back into town laughing mockingly. Sister Luna broke into tears crying at the sight in front of her. Trying desperately not to cry, Mother Lucrezia and Siobhan lifted her up and carried her to her room.

They placed her gently on her bed, then Mother Lucrezia ran out of the room to get the first aid kit. Siobhan stared down at Sister Garcia in horror and grief. She could tell just by looking at her that Sister Garcia was going to die. Mother Lucrezia returned with a first aid kit quickly.

"Get out of the room!" barked Mother Lucrezia.

Siobhan obediently stepped out of the room and closed the door behind her. For the next hour, Siobhan sat with Sister Luna consoling her as best she could in the kitchen. Mother Lucrezia walked into the room, the look on her face dashing any hopes Sister Luna might have of Sister Garcia survival.

"I'm sorry, she's with the Lord now," said Mother Lucrezia delicately.

In response, Sister Luna buried her face in her hands sobbing uncontrollably. Mother Lucrezia and Siobhan sat next to her and held her.

That night, as Sister Luna cried herself to sleep and Mother Lucrezia prayed for Sister Garcia's soul, Siobhan was in her room sitting on the edge of her bed unable to sleep. She buried her face in her hands consumed by grief. Then the grief passed, replaced by righteous indignation. She was shaking ever so slightly as if her body could not contain the rage as it struggled to escape.

Chapter 10

Up from the Fire

After deciding to bury Sister Garcia behind the convent in the morning, Sister Luna asked to be alone. Mother Lucrezia and Siobhan nodded understandingly as she stood up and walked to her room. Siobhan noticed that Sister Luna had an almost dazed look on her face. Lucrezia and Siobhan left the kitchen shortly after Sister Luna.

As Siobhan walked back to her room, her grief slowly turned to anger once more. Once inside she closed the door behind her. Finally, she could control her rage no longer and punched the wall with all her strength leaving a hole, staring back at her. Her knuckles were bruised from the punch but she ignored the pain. She stared at the hole for a few seconds, her mind racing.

She shifted her gaze to the mirror, her eyes locked on her reflection; she got on her knees and began to pray.

"Lord, what should I do, why punish these people for my sins? These are kind people who don't deserve this," said Siobhan as she clutched her hands together.

Suddenly as if in answer, Siobhan heard an explosion followed by a burst of machine gun fire in the distance.

It was as if her two lives, her old life as an assassin and her new life as a nun, had collided in that moment. As she listened to the sounds echo in the distance, she had an epiphany. Finally, her most burning questions were answered: the reason for her nightmares, why she felt compelled to practice her fighting skills, and why she kept that trunk — all of them were answered. God was not punishing her as she previously thought. Instead, he had given her a new purpose: to atone for her sins by avenging his fallen children, starting with Sister Garcia's murderers.

She stood up, tilted her head upwards, closed her eyes, and whispered "Thank you."

"No longer will I be a devil but an avenging angel, an Angel of Vengeance," she thought. Siobhan stood up, walked over to her bed purposefully, and pulled her chest out from under it. If I am to be an instrument of the Lord's divine wrath, then so be it, thought Siobhan. She quickly entered the combination on the lock and opened the chest.

Inside the chest staring back at her were several kinds of knives, two Colt M1911 semiautomatic pistols, a double vertical holster for the pistols, sawed off double barrel shotgun, ammunition, a suppressor and a disassembled AK-47, her preferred assault rifle.

She had stolen them from an IRA safe house in case she ever needed them. After checking the weapons to make sure they were in good condition, she decided to attack the FARC at night under the cover of darkness. In the darkness of night, she hoped to instill in them the same terror they had inflicted on Sister Garcia. She briefly considered wearing the combat suit inside, but decided against it.

The woman who wore that uniform was dead and was reborn as an angel of vengeance. She closed the chest, slid it back under the bed, and set her alarm clock to wake her up around midnight. She undressed and then got into bed and slept.

When the alarm beeped, she awoke and shut it off quickly. As she got out of bed, she glanced at her habit, hanging in her closet, and suddenly realized that her black and white nun habit would make perfect armor. Since none of the guerillas would expect danger from someone dressed as a nun, and as it was almost all black, she would be hard to see. It also felt appropriate to wear it on her crusade because Sister Garcia also wore a habit in her last moments. She put it on and then shifted her attention to the chest under her bed.

She pulled the chest out from under the bed, opened it, and put on her knife belt, which could hold up to three knifes. Then she slid on her double cross-draw shoulder holster. She picked up her pistols, loaded them and screwed on the silencers, then casually slid them into the holsters. She grabbed three of the knives and put them in her knife belt. Finally, she went to her closet and put on her black overcoat to hide her weapons.

She took a deep breath, wondering whether or not her skills had faded with time, then walked over to the window. She opened the window and slid out into the ethereal blackness of the night, making sure to close it. She turned around and saw Malvara in the distance, the town looked quiet and serene. Unfortunately, it sounded very different with the occasional machine gun burst and terrified scream. Siobhan began to walk into town casually so as not to arouse any suspicion in case someone would see her.

Upon entering Malvara, she was not surprised but angry to see that the guerillas had wrecked the town. As she walked, she could see the windows were cracked and several buildings reduced to rubble. It reminded her of the aftermath of a brutal riot she had witnessed as a child in Belfast between rioters and British soldiers. As she surveyed the destruction, her resolve to avenge Sister Garcia and the murdered townspeople only grew stronger.

As she continued walking, she felt a hand place itself roughly on her shoulder, stopping her. "Where do you think you're going?" said the man in Spanish.

Siobhan could tell he was a FARC soldier by his voice. She grinned confident that her abilities had not diminished. The man asked again impatiently as he tightened his grip on her shoulder. Siobhan placed her hand on the man's hand gently. Before he could respond, she crushed his hand. She could hear the faint cracking of the man's bones.

As the man began to howl in pain, Siobhan reached into her belt, pulled out a knife, spun around, and slashed the man across his throat. The look on his face as blood began to pour out of the gash across his neck was one of shock and terror, then nothing. He fell on the sidewalk, dead. As Siobhan wiped the blood off her knife on the man's pants, she noticed that he was carrying a Dragunov sniper rifle, a two-way radio, and a pouch with a block of C4 inside. She slid the knife back into its sheath on her belt. Then she slung the pouch over her shoulder, put the radio in her pocket, and picked up the rifle.

She held the radio to her ear and heard the men talking about a command post being in the town hall. Stealthily, she made her way there. Parked in front of it on the sidewalk was an armored car. Inside a guard was half-asleep at the wheel. Siobhan snuck up to him and tapped on the window. Drowsily the driver looked toward her. Siobhan punched the window, shattered it in one blow, pulled out a knife, and stabbed the driver in the throat with it.

She pulled out the C4 and tossed it in the car; then she wrote a note on the pouch in the man's blood and pinned it to the driver's body. Her task half-completed, Siobhan ran across the street and climbed to the top of one of the buildings. She screwed the suppressor onto the barrel of the Dragunov and lay down on the roof aiming at the window of the town hall. She fired a few shots at the window, shattering it and bringing several guerillas running outside. What they saw was the driver of one of their armored cars dead with a pouch of C4 pinned to his body.

Upon closer inspection, they noticed that the pouch had writing on it in Spanish. It read:

Leave now or answer for your sins.
The Angel of Vengeance

Siobhan watched as they laughed at the note. They had made their choice, thought Siobhan. With the block of C4 in her sights, she fired at it causing it to explode, killing most of the guerillas, and wounding a few. Siobhan tossed the Dragunov aside and climbed down from the building. She could hear other guerillas approaching, having heard the explosion.

Satisfied with her work, she retreated into the darkness of the night and stealthily made her way back to the Convent before anyone knew what happened.

Chapter 11

Concrete Hunting Ground

The next morning they buried Sister Garcia in a grave behind the convent. The service was short and touching, Sister Luna's face was consumed by tears as Mother Lucrezia, impassive as ever, spoke. Sister Luna left the service in tears while Mother Lucrezia held back hers. Siobhan however, heard none of Mother Lucrezias eulogy as it was drowned out by the memory of what she had done the night before. After the service, they retreated to their rooms.

Last night Siobhan had killed around nine FARC guerillas and left their bodies bleeding on the street for their comrades to find. Ordinarily she would be in the depths of despair because of the men she had killed, angry at herself for breaking her promise. Instead, she was quite content, at peace even. It was as if her epiphany last night had gifted her with an inner peace she hadn't known since she was a young child. What most calmed her though was the new sense of purpose she had found: delivering God's wrath to those who killed his children as an angel of vengeance.

She spent the remainder of the day planning how to get the FARC guerillas out of Malvara while doing her daily chores. She had decided that every night, once her fellow sisters had gone to bed, she would go out into Malvara and kill as many of them as she could, until they left the town. The only thing that scared her was her fellow sisters finding out what she did at night. What she couldn't determine was whether or not to stay in Malvara once the FARC threat was dealt with. When she was in the IRA, she had heard of an island called Sankan in the Philippine Sea, ruled by criminals and sin.

She briefly considered leaving the convent when the FARC threat was dealt with. But she discarded the idea of leaving Malvara as Mother Lucrezia and Sister Luna had become like family to her and she was not about to abandon another family. The rest of the day went on as usual, as the nuns went about their duties as best they could. The three of them went to bed at the same time as usual. At midnight, however she awoke, put on her weapons and nuns habit and snuck out the window. She noticed that wearing the habit felt right, like it was meant to be.

As she began walking in to town, confident she was doing the right thing, she noticed the full moon in the sky basking Malvara in a hauntingly beautiful glow. It was as if God was giving her permission to do what she was about to do. As she walked through town, she passed two FARC soldiers who despite their best efforts looked nervous. Siobhan could tell that their nervousness was a result of discovering the bodies of the men she killed the night before. The look of smug arrogance on their faces had been replaced with fear.

She saw them try to hide their fear and she felt a sense of satisfaction deep within her that manifested in a sly grin. Is it wrong to take pride in killing these men, she pondered. So caught up was she in her thoughts that she didn't notice she was in the alley between Armando's bar and the town inn. Upon realizing where she was, she turned to leave when the back door of the bar opened and three drunken FARC guerillas walked out laughing. However, once they saw Siobhan, they stopped and grinned sadistically.

Siobhan could tell what their intentions were and she tensed herself in readiness for a fight. Thought left her as she studied them as the three men walked toward her menacingly.

"I'll go first," muttered the man closest to her.

"As you wish," replied Siobhan calmly.

Before they could even blink, Siobhan pulled out a knife and jammed it into the man's stomach. He immediately bent over in pain clutching his bleeding stomach. Before the other two men could react Siobhan quickly pulled out one of her silenced .45 pistols and shot them both in the forehead. As the other man looked back up at Siobhan, he lunged at her in rage. Siobhan grabbed him by his collar with her free hand and slammed his face into the side of the building.

She quickly looked around for any witnesses and breathed a sigh of relief when she didn't see any. She holstered her pistol and checked the man for any pulse, there was none. Calmly and quickly, she walked out of the alley, listening intently for anything dangerous. Within minutes, Siobhan was far enough away from the alley. As she continued walking down the streets, she saw two FARC soldiers beating an old man in the street.

Her blood boiling with rage, she calmly and quietly walked up to them. She noticed that one of them had a GM-94 grenade launcher slung over his shoulder. Approaching them at the far end of the street was a jeep with four FARC guerillas in it. Siobhan ran up behind the guerilla holding the grenade launcher and plunged her knife into the back of his neck. Before the other guerilla could react, Siobhan drew her pistol and fired two shots at him.

She picked up the grenade launcher, aimed it at the approaching jeep, and fired a grenade at the jeep. The grenade exploded on contact with the car; instinctively she slung the grenade launcher over her shoulder. She turned to help the old man when suddenly two strong arms wrapped around her waist roughly in an attempt to restrain her. Siobhan crushed his foot with hers causing his grip on her to loosen. She took advantage of the moment, spun around, and struck him in the neck with a karate chop.

Instinctively he grabbed his throat while Siobhan hit him in the stomach with her left knee. Finally, she grabbed him by his collar and threw him to the ground, pulled out her Colt and shot him twice in the back. She felt slightly embarrassed that he had managed to get that close to her in the first place. She could hear more guerillas approaching attracted by the noise like moths to a flame. She knelt down and checked the old man; he was alive, just unconscious.

Siobhan picked him up, put him over her shoulder, and ran down the street into an alley. She laid the old man on the ground behind a dumpster where, she hoped, he would be safe from the FARC. She was about to leave when she remembered the grenade launcher and an idea crossed her mind. She grinned softly at the idea and decided to go through with it since the night was still young.

*****

A half hour later Commander Sandoval sat in his makeshift office in the town hall. The building was in shambles after the bombing of the previous night. They had spent the whole day cleaning it up and it was almost done, which made up for the fact that it was bombed in the first place. Sandoval sat in his chair wracking his brains trying to figure how these people pulled it off. But that was not the only thing on his mind this night. When he heard that, his men had raped and killed a nun in a fit of drunkenness he almost flew into a rage.

Like many in his homeland, he grew up in a poor neighborhood to Catholic parents. The church represented hope and salvation for his parents. However, when his family died of a disease that could have been treated, had they been wealthy. He became distant from the church. It was at this time in his life that he learned of the FARC. As a young man, he was attracted to their promises of a Columbia where all were equal regardless of wealth. In the FARC, he was taught that soldiers must be given leave to remain effective, and that religion was used to enslave the working class.

However, he had childhood memories of the church helping his family, which contradicted the rhetoric drilled into him by the FARC's leadership. He had never been in a position like this, where his men had committed such a heinous action and were so badly needed. As he sat, there in his office contemplating how to deal with them he was unaware of a woman planting herself across the street from his headquarters with a grenade launcher.

Sandoval rubbed his face tired and frustrated. He got out of his desk chair and made his way to the bed, when suddenly the building shook as a loud cacophonous explosion erupted outside. Instantly, the building was a hive of activity as his men woke up and scrambled to find who was behind this latest attack.

Siobhan tossed the grenade launcher to the ground as smoke wafted from its barrel. Rather than staying to watch, she chose to disappear into the shadows. She decided she had done enough for that night and made her way back to the convent.

Chapter 12

BOG

Despite his best efforts, Mendelsohn arrived at El Dorado International airport in Bogota Colombia jet lagged. Upon recovering his luggage and leaving the terminal, he was greeted by an Interpol agent.

"Welcome to Colombia, agent Mendelsohn," said the agent as they shook hands. "Right this way."

Mendelsohn followed the agent to his car in the parking lot. "Where are we going first, the hotel or the office?" he asked hoping for the former.

"I've been instructed to take you straight to the Interpol building, the boss wants to speak to you ASAP," replied the agent.

"Great," muttered Mendelsohn, slightly irritated, since all he wanted right now was some sleep.

Upon arrival at the Interpol building, Mendelsohn followed the agent inside. The Interpol building was dwarfed in size by the building across the street from it: a skyscraper belonging to an international bank named King Midas Holdings. After Mendelsohn handed his weapon over to security, they walked across the lobby to the elevator.

"The boss is in his office, on the top floor," said the agent and stopped in front of the elevator to push the button.

"Thanks for the ride," replied Mendelsohn as he entered the elevator. The agent nodded in response.

In a few minutes, Mendelsohn arrived at the top floor and was escorted to the office of the head of Interpol activities in Colombia— Director Manuel Gaspar.

Mendelsohn knocked on the door and after hearing a muffled "come in" walked inside.

The office had a bookshelf on the left wall and several pictures on the walls of Gaspar receiving medals. In the center of the room was a desk with a chair in front of it. Sitting behind the desk was Director Gaspar; he was surprisingly fit for a man his age. He had a large black mustache and was dressed in a casual suit. Gaspar looked up from the computer on his desk and stood up as Mendelsohn walked in.

"Welcome, Agent Mendelsohn, how was your flight?" he asked.

"I've had worse," Mendelssohn, answered as they shook hands.

Gaspar laughed, "Haven't we all? Please, have a seat," he said gesturing to the seat in front of his desk.

Mendelsohn sat in the chair comfortably. "Did you get my message about Costello?" asked Mendelsohn, wishing to get down to business.

"Yes I did, and I'm sure that I'm not the only person to tell you this, but the likelihood of her being alive after all this time is hard to believe," Gaspar replied. "I especially find it hard to believe that she is hiding out here, especially considering the source, this Tierney, who's a convicted terrorist. What makes you think he's telling the truth?" he continued.

"Call it a hunch," answered Mendelsohn.

Gaspar stared at him for almost a full minute. "Fair enough. Still, I looked into this Malvara, and while it does exist, there's a problem."

"There usually is," said Mendelsohn sardonically. "What is it?" he asked, sensing that he wasn't going to like it.

"Several days ago an army of FARC guerillas invaded the town and seized control of it," answered Gaspar.

Mendelssohn raised his eyebrow in surprise. "I thought that the FARC disarmed after the peace treaty."

Gaspar sighed, "I wish that it were so easy, but sadly between two thousand and twenty-five hundred, of their forces have refused to disarm and surrender. Most of them have fled the country and became hired guns for the Rojas Cartel in Brazil or crossed the border into Venezuela, but most of them are still continuing the fight or joined local cartels."

Mendelsohn sighed at Gaspar's news since it was worse than he had expected. He assumed the biggest problem would be getting help from local law enforcement but this would require military help. She's probably joined the bastards, thought Mendelssohn, remembering what he read in her file.

"As for Malvara, they've claimed it as a garrison and effectively sealed it off from the outside world," continued Gaspar.

"Damn, that is bad," replied Mendelsohn.

"However, I contacted a friend in the ANIC and found out some things that might help us," said Gaspar.

"What is it?" asked Mendelsohn curious as to what this silver lining might be.

"At night they've been flying drones over the town for reconnaissance for when the army liberates the town and they saw something very interesting the last few nights," Gaspar answered as he opened a manila folder on his desk and pulled out a picture. "I got this from my friend, I think you might find it interesting," said Gaspar as he handed it to Mendelsohn.

Mendelsohn accepted the picture and studied it; the photo was zoomed in on the main street in the town at night. However, what stuck out was the burning wreckage of a car and what looked like a female figure walking away from it, with several bodies of what Mendelsohn assumed were civilians behind her.

"This was taken by a drone last night," said Gaspar as Mendelsohn studied the photo.

"According to my contact at the ANIC, on every one of the recon flights the drones picked up that woman, dressed as a nun, attacking the FARC guerillas brutally," Gaspar added. "According to my friend, who has seen this video, this woman is extremely well-trained and brutal in her attacks."

He concluded, "Unfortunately we can't seem to identify this person, but based on what they saw, her training matches that of this Shopan woman."

"It's actually Siobhan, but why would she attack the FARC?" responded Mendelsohn.

Gaspar shrugged, "I don't know, but that's not even the strangest thing, according to my friend," answered Gaspar.

"Oh?" questioned Mendelsohn.

"Whoever she is, she always returns to a convent at the edge of town."

"You must be joking?" said Mendelsohn as he looked up from the photo.

"It gets even stranger, the army has been listening to radio chatter among the guerillas referring to this woman as the Angel of Vengeance," said Gaspar.

"Now I know your joking, the Angel of Vengeance? Seriously, what is this? A comic book?" said Mendelsohn almost laughing.

"I never joke about my work," Gaspar replied.

"I see. Well, it's funny because according to her file Siobhan is believed to be a devout Irish Catholic," said Barry.

"Awfully coincidental, isn't it?" observed Gaspar.

"Either way, we'll need some help to get in there and prove it's her doing this," said Mendelsohn.

"Well, my friend in the AINC told me that the army is planning to invade Malvara and retake it very soon."

"Excellent. Can you send me in with them?" asked Mendelsohn.

"My friend in the AINC owes me a great many favors, so I could convince him to let you accompany the commandos into Malvara," answered Gaspar. He continued, "However you won't be able to arrest her; the army will arrest her."

"We'll have to notify the British Embassy once we have her so she can be extradited," said Mendelsohn.

"True, but I must warn you this will be dangerous. Are you sure you want to go?" asked Gaspar.

"I can take care of myself, besides I've spent too much time tracking her to let someone else get her," answered Mendelsohn.

"I can understand that, I'll make the arrangements."

"When did your friend say it'll be?" Mendelsohn inquired.

"He didn't tell me but I can find out. Now that we have dispensed with business I have a question," said Gaspar. "I was about to go out to eat when you arrived; would you like to come?"

"If it's not an imposition," replied Mendelsohn politely.

"Nonsense, you are a guest in my country, come let's go," said Gaspar with a smile.

"If you insist," said Mendelsohn.

As Gaspar and Mendelsohn left the ICPO building, they were unaware that their conversation had been overheard by men in two cars across the street. One of the cars contained members of the Triad who had just sent the conversation to Sankan Island to be analyzed. The other car belonged to the Order of the Silent Disciple's; its occupants had just transmitted it to their superiors in Vatican City. Their mission accomplished, they returned to their respective headquarters.

*****

Two hours later on Sankan Island, Mazin walked into Deng's office carrying a transcript of the conversation.

"Well, Mazin, this better be good," said Deng as Mazin came in.

"It is, read this," said Mazin and he handed the transcript to Deng.

Deng spent the next several minutes quickly reading it.

"This is from our team in Bogota. They found out Mendelsohn had arrived there and followed him to the ICPO building," said Mazin as Deng read it.

Deng returned the transcript to Mazin. "It sounds farfetched but keep me updated," said Deng. "Any word yet on the Velvet Dragon incident?"

"Nothing new, the police think it was a hit by a rival gang," answered Mazin.

"Of course they do," said Deng dismissively. "Does the Mountain Master know about it?"

"Yes, he's spoken to the Russians and the Italians; it wasn't them," answered Mazin.

"Whoever it was knew what they were doing and what they were looking for," said Deng.

"Do you think it was the Networc?" asked Mazin.

"No, it's too small for them. Either way we have more important things to deal with," said Deng. "Any word from Simon and Mai?"

"No sir."

"I didn't think there was," said Deng.

*****

Commander Sandoval stood outside surveying the damage of last night's attack on his headquarters, growing angrier at the sight of each piece of rubble. Cautiously, one of his aides walked up to him and meekly addressed him. Sandoval turned around to see what he wanted.

"Sir, we found someone who knows who did this," said the soldier.

"Is that so?" Sandoval replied.

"Yes sir. An old man who was rescued by the attacker was found behind a dumpster and interrogated," the soldier explained.

"I see. And what did he say?" Sandoval asked.

"It was a nun from the convent outside of town," answered the soldier.

I'm not surprised, we took one of theirs, and they want justice, he thought. "Ready the men, we're going to the convent," ordered Sandoval.

Chapter 13

Closing In For the Kill

After three days, Siobhan noticed a curious new occurrence in the FARC guerillas in town: there were less of them patrolling the streets at night. Siobhan knew why: it was fear, the fear of facing judgment. She had also noticed that Sister Luna's mood had improved as a result of being counseled by Mother Lucrezia and herself. Twice a day she would place flowers on Sister Garcia's grave. Siobhan had begun to feel more and more pleased with herself when she returned to the convent each night.

Perhaps as a result of her nocturnal rampages she had begun carrying a knife on her at all times, hidden under her clothes.

During the days, she had devoted more time to her reading of scripture in the lobby of the convent. Mother Lucrezia, she noticed, remained as cool and aloof as usual. Though one thing Siobhan could never figure out was how Mother Lucrezia was able to sneak up on her without her noticing. But, she had long since abandoned the idea of trying to understand Mother Lucrezia. As far as Siobhan could tell, both Sister Luna and Mother Lucrezia were unaware of her nocturnal activities.

The Colombian Army convoy sped down the road. It was comprised of four gun trucks, a tank, four trucks loaded with soldiers, and a jeep in front. Sitting in the jeep was agent Barry Mendelsohn. It took three days but Gaspar had come through, Mendelsohn made a note to thank him for this and the dinner. Mendelsohn glanced down at his bulletproof vest and couldn't help but be reminded of his time in the Canadian army. In the back of the jeep were two heavily armed Colombian army soldiers.

The plan was to arrest Siobhan, while the gun trucks went into town and confronted the

FARC forces. Upon entering the town, the convoy was greeted by a hail of machine gun fire from the rooftops and the streets. Mendelsohn instinctively pulled out his Beretta as he ducked below the dashboard. He was just about to return fire when the driver made a hard left turn away from the town.

"What the hell?" asked Mendelsohn annoyed at the sudden turn.

The driver looked at him, a surly confused look on his face, and pointed in front of him. Mendelsohn shifted his gaze to what he was pointing at.

"Oh," said Mendelsohn feeling stupid as they drew closer to the convent.

"That is what you seek yes?" asked the driver.

"It's whose inside that really interests me," replied Mendelsohn.

Inside the convent, the nuns were looking out the window to investigate the noise.

"Who's that driving up to us in that jeep," asked Sister Luna pointing to it.

"Looks like an army jeep," answered Mother Lucrezia.

Siobhan tensed up nervously fearing that it was the guerillas.

The jeep pulled up in front of the convent and Mendelsohn and the two soldiers in the back disembarked while the driver stayed in the jeep. Mendelsohn and the soldiers began approaching the convent.

"Hey Sister Darcy, who's that man in the suit carrying the pistol," asked Sister Luna pointing to Mendelsohn.

"I don't know," answered Siobhan, relieved that it wasn't the guerillas. Siobhan tensed nervously.

Mendelsohn knocked on the door demanding in Spanish that they open it.

Sister Luna opened it and Barry Mendelsohn walked in. Standing right in front of him at long last was Siobhan. He could not believe that the nun was the woman Lohman had showed him in the picture, and that she was actually standing in front of him. However, the likeness was the same. Mendelsohn pulled out his Beretta and aimed it at her, suddenly remembering what Nigel had said.

"That's her. Arrest her!" barked Barry as he motioned to the soldiers.

"Who are you?" Sister Luna demanded.

With his free hand, he reached into his pocket, pulled out his Interpol badge, and showed it to her.

His words hit Siobhan like a sledgehammer, while the two soldiers looked at each other confused; however, they followed their orders and placed handcuffs on her wrists. As Siobhan stood handcuffed, she asked herself how this could have happened.

Sister Luna and Mother Lucrezia watched incredulously.

"Why are you arresting Sister Darcy? The guerillas are out there," shouted Sister Luna.

Mendelsohn turned to face them suddenly remembering that they were there.

"Sister Darcy? Sisters, I don't know who you think this woman is, but her real name is Siobhan Costello," answered Mendelsohn. "She's a wanted terrorist, known as the Devil Woman, wanted in over a dozen countries for terrorism, theft, and outright murder."

The words echoed in Siobhan's head like a shockwave as he said them. Siobhan hung her head, too ashamed to look at Sister Luna and Mother Lucrezia.

"Sister Darcy, this can't be true. Tell me it isn't," said Sister Luna, tears welling up in her eyes.

"I'm sorry but it is true, I am guilty of all those things and more, but I left that behind. I came here seeking redemption," said Siobhan as she too had tears in her eyes.

"You can talk later," interrupted Mendelsohn.

The soldiers grabbed her by her arms and began escorting her to the door. Suddenly something inside her snapped as the soldiers put their hands on her. Siobhan managed to free herself from the handcuffs. She kicked one of the soldiers in the chest, knocking him to the ground. Then she hit the other soldier in the stomach with her elbow and knocked him to the ground with the back of her hand

"Freeze," yelled Mendelsohn as he put his pistol against the back of her head.

Siobhan stood still; she could hear it click as he pulled back the hammer. Before Mendelsohn knew what happened, she had turned around facing him. She grabbed the wrist of his gun hand and twisted it causing him to drop the gun; then she punched him in the nose, knocking him to the floor. Quickly, she walked over to one of the unconscious soldiers, pulled out a ring of keys, and removed the handcuffs. Siobhan turned around to face her sisters; Sister Luna was looking at her, her face a contortion of fear, shock, and anger, while Mother Lucrezia looked on as impassive as ever.

"I don't know what to say, other than I am sorry for deceiving you all this time," said Siobhan.

"You've killed before, you've lied to us. Now you have killed three men in God's house, and now you dare expect our forgiveness?" barked Sister Luna.

Siobhan bent her head in shame as she listened to Sister Luna's recriminations. In a way, it was a relief to have her secret revealed. Siobhan still felt mortified, as her worst nightmare had become reality.

Chapter 14

Nowhere to Run

Sister Luna's words echoed in Siobhan's mind until she fell to her knees and began sobbing uncontrollably.

"Mother Lucrezia, Sister Luna. Please forgive me," Siobhan pleaded.

Mother Lucrezia gently put her hand on Siobhan's shoulder.

"Rise my dear, I know you feel ashamed of what you have done in the past. However, since you came here. I have sensed a strong desire for redemption in you. God has seen that in you as well, and that's why you're here," said Mother Lucrezia comfortingly.

Siobhan stood up feeling better and her tears stopped.

Mother Lucrezia then shifted her gaze to Sister Luna scolding her. "Sister Luna how dare you, she is still the same kind and compassionate woman we've known all these years regardless of her past sins and none of us are without sin," she said.

"What about those men on the ground she killed?" Sister Luna asked.

"They aren't dead."

Siobhan and Sister Luna looked at Mother Lucrezia confused over how she knew they were still alive.

"How do you know that?" asked Sister Luna.

"They're still breathing," Mother Lucrezia, answered gesturing to the men. "Besides I was watching you, Sister Darcy, or should I say Costello. You didn't hit them hard enough to kill them though I know you could have, if you had wanted to."

Before any of them could say another word, they were interrupted by a burst of machine gun fire, the howl of several cars coming to a halt and the scream of a man being killed outside. They looked out in horror to see two FARC trucks parked in front of the convent. In front of the trucks stood several FARC guerillas and lying on the ground motionless in a pool of his own blood was the driver.

Their leader stood up from his seat in the back of the lead jeep. He raised a bullhorn to his mouth.

"Surrender the interlopers to us or die in pieces," yelled Sandoval through the bullhorn.

The nuns stared at each other unsure of what to do. Mother Lucrezia walked to the window.

"You come to this village and turn it into a war zone. You will not do the same to this building!" yelled Mother Lucrezia, her voice getting louder with each word.

She reached into her pocket and pulled out a .44 Magnum revolver. She aimed it at the man with the bullhorn and fired one bullet at him. His head flew back and he fell backward onto the ground. As the gunshot echoed around them, Mother Lucrezia grabbed the two doors of the convent and slammed them shut. She locked the door, as Siobhan and Sister Luna looked on in shock, their minds trying to make sense of what they had just seen. Mother Lucrezia, sensing the questions in their minds, smiled.

"Claire, my dear, you aren't the only one with a secret. Let's just say in my youth I belonged to a certain order in Vatican City," said Mother Lucrezia.

Suddenly a machine gun burst shattered the window. Instinctively Siobhan jumped to the ground and yelled, "Get down!" Sister Luna and Mother Lucrezia jumped behind a table.

"Siobhan, get the guns in your room," yelled Mother Lucrezia.

Siobhan was about to ask how she knew about the guns, but instead nodded and ran to her room. Just as Siobhan left, Mendelsohn awoke.

"What the hell?" yelled Mendelsohn upon hearing the commotion of bullets bouncing off the exterior of the building.

He quickly searched the room for Siobhan but saw nothing. Mother Lucrezia was in his face in minutes. She grabbed him by his jacket.

"Interpol agent, she is not your problem at the moment, they are," said Mother Lucrezia, pointing to the guerillas outside. "If you arrest her now we all die, make a choice."

Mendelsohn looked out the window then back at Mother Lucrezia.

"You make a hell of an argument, Sister," said Mendelsohn, having decided to arrest Siobhan when this was over.

"I thought so," said Mother Lucrezia as she let him go.

Mendelsohn picked up his pistol, holstered it, ran over to one of the unconscious soldiers, and picked up his IMI Galil rifle. Mendelsohn aimed it out the window and began firing short bursts at the attacking FARC commandos. When Siobhan returned to the room, the first thing she saw was Mendelsohn, conscious, shooting at the guerillas alongside Mother Lucrezia. She ignored him but kept an eye on him as she set the chest on the floor and opened it. Mother Lucrezia ran over to it. Holstering her pistol, she reached inside and grabbed the shotgun.

Siobhan pulled out the AK-47 and quickly began assembling it. Mendelsohn looked over and noticed the seemingly bottomless amount of guns, knives, and bullets in the trunk.

"How many guns do you have?" asked Mendelsohn as he reloaded.

"Enough" answered Siobhan as she put in a fresh magazine.

She cocked the rifle, then ran over to another window and began firing at the guerillas.

Sister Luna looked up from behind the table scared and feeling more useless now than in her entire life. Siobhan fired short bursts at the FARC commandos, who were taking cover behind the trucks. Suddenly one of them stood up holding a round gray object in his right hand ready to throw it.

Siobhan instantly knew what it was, aimed right for it as she squinted one of her eyes, and yelled, "Grenade!"

Mendelsohn and Mother Lucrezia ducked and covered their ears.

Siobhan fired at the grenade, praying her aim was still as good as it used to be. Her bullet hit the grenade and the subsequent explosion caused the other four grenades on the man's belt to explode. The magnified explosion also caused one of the trucks to explode killing a large number of the guerillas. When the dust had settled Siobhan, Mendelsohn and Mother Lucrezia looked out the window and smiled the smile of the victorious.

The remaining FARC guerillas were running as fast as they could from the convent only to be caught and ultimately arrested by the Army.

Mother Lucrezia sat down feeling and looking exhausted.

"I haven't been in a fight like that since the 70s," said Mother Lucrezia. They all laughed at her comment, taking solace in victory.

"Well, Siobhan, I got to hand it to you, that was a hell of a shot but I have a job to do," said Mendelsohn and aimed his pistol at her.

Instinctively Siobhan tensed herself in readiness to attack him.

"Don't move," said Mendelsohn as he approached her.

She stared at him with a glare that could melt steel. "What are you doing, you can't arrest me," Siobhan asked bluntly.

"You're right, I can't but the reinforcements we called for can and they will," explained Barry.

Before Siobhan could reply, Mendelsohn fell to the ground unconscious.

Standing above him, holding the butt of one of the soldier's rifles, was Sister Luna. "I forgive you, Sister Darcy," she said.

After everything that had happened in the last few days, Siobhan didn't think she was still capable of being surprised or forgiven.

Siobhan smiled, "thank you, Sister Luna."

"Siobhan, you must leave now," said Mother Lucrezia, her sternness having returned.

"Mother Lucrezia, she helped," said Sister Luna.

"Hush," interrupted Mother Lucrezia raising her hand. "What do you think he will do when he awakens?" she asked Siobhan, gesturing to Mendelsohn's unconscious body.

"You're right, but where will I go? What will I do? This church is all I have," protested Siobhan.

"No, you have something better than this church," said Mother Lucrezia. "You have a new purpose, my dear, to walk the Earth and be God's silent avenger, destroying those evil and wicked souls who kill and maim the innocent."

"But what if they return?"

"Nonsense, these men will never return here after what happened," said Mother Lucrezia.

Siobhan thought about everything Mother Lucrezia had said and knew she was right. "Alright, I'll go," she said. "But what about him," gesturing to the unconscious body of Barry Mendelsohn lying face first on the floor.

"We'll take care of him," answered Mother Lucrezia comfortingly.

"But why, he'll come after you," said Sister Luna impertinently.

"You're more right than you know, Sister, but there's been enough death and killing today," said Siobhan regretfully.

Sister Luna helped her pack some clothes and a few guns into a suitcase. Before leaving, she gave Sister Luna a tearful hug goodbye.

"Sister Darcy, I want you to have this," said Sister Lucrezia as she removed her gold necklace with a cross on it.

Before Siobhan could speak a word of protest, Lucrezia held up her hand. "It will remind you of your mission and the salvation that lies beyond," she said.

"Thank you," said Siobhan feeling honored as she put the necklace on.

"Before you go, here's something else for you," said Mother Lucrezia, as she reached into her pocket, pulled out an envelope, and handed it to her.

"What is this?" asked Siobhan.

"Travel expenses," Mother Lucrezia answered.

Siobhan opened it and saw that there was over one thousand and two hundred pesos in cash inside. She put the envelope in her pocket and hugged Mother Lucrezia, as both of them had tears forming in their eyes.

"Good luck on your mission, and avoid Disciple 13; you don't need them," whispered Mother Lucrezia.

Siobhan didn't know what Disciple 13 was but had a feeling she would find out someday. As they let each other go, Siobhan looked at them one last time.

"Goodbye," said Siobhan tearfully.

She walked to the jeep Mendelsohn arrived in, placed her suitcase in the back, and looked at the convent one last time with tears in her eyes. She looked away, started the car before crying again, and then drove off out of Malvara.

*****

Four hours later Mendelsohn and the soldiers woke up; Mendelsohn found himself lying in a bed, Mother Lucrezia and Sister Luna staring at him harshly. His arm had been bandaged and was in a sling much to his surprise.

"Careful, you've been shot," said Mother Lucrezia.

Upon recovering his faculties, Mendelsohn looked for Siobhan but saw nothing.

"I managed to remove the bullet but I recommend you go to the hospital," said Mother Lucrezia.

Mendelsohn looked angrily at Sister Luna, "You! You knocked me out so she could escape." Mendelsohn was furious.

"You can't prove anything and you know it," said Mother Lucrezia smugly. "Be realistic, what are you going to tell your superiors in Lyon? That you were knocked out by three nuns after fighting an army of FARC guerillas? You'll be committed," she said with a sly grin that only infuriated Mendelsohn more.

She was right and Mendelsohn knew it, though he was determined to have the last word. "You know, when you put it like that, it does sound kind of stupid," said Mendelsohn.

"It would make an interesting movie, though," chirped Sister Luna grinning at his frustration and bruised ego.

Mendelsohn stood up and walked to the door. "Be that as it may, she can't hide. I will find her, and if not me then someone else. A person with her past has more enemies than friends," said Mendelsohn.

"Then it's a good thing she has a head start," responded Mother Lucrezia.

Realizing that he had been outmaneuvered, Mendelsohn decided to leave.

"Be seeing you," said Mendelsohn as he and the soldiers turned to leave.

Once they were out of the convent, Mendelsohn turned to one of the soldiers.

"How long until we can establish contact with Bogota," he asked in Spanish.

The soldier looked at him quizzically. "Around four hours, answered the man in Spanish.

"Dammit," muttered Mendelsohn.

She's got an eight-hour head start; that's long enough for her to get out of the country, thought Mendelsohn.

What made matters worse was that she knew Interpol and MI6 would be coming after her. She knew she had to hide.

Still Mendelsohn was up for the challenge.

Chapter 15

Back in the World

Siobhan arrived at El Dorado International Airport only to be faced with a new dilemma: where to go. She sat in the jeep and thought about all the places she could flee to. Suddenly she realized where she should go: a place ruled by sin and evil, the island of Sankan. There she could continue her crusade. Unfortunately, because of its size and obscurity, no airlines flew to it directly but she was determined to go there anyway. She stepped out of the jeep and entered the airport.

The only available flight that she could afford was a flight to Sydney Airport in Australia. She shrugged, deciding to transfer to a flight to the Philippines. When she arrived at Sydney, she would charter a boat to Sankan. She quickly bought a ticket and got something to eat at a small restaurant in the airport while she waited. As Siobhan sat at the table and watched the people walk about the airport, she felt strange being in the outside world again.

After a few hours of waiting in the terminal, she boarded the plane unaware that she had just triggered a flurry of activity on opposite sides of the globe.

From the moment she entered the airport, she had been watched surreptitiously by agents of Disciple 13 and the Heise She Li Triad. The agents quickly notified their respective superiors of this development as per the orders.

In Vatican City, after being told of Siobhan's status by his assistant Reno, Bishop Marzano thought for a minute. He looked up at Reno and told him, "Reno, send Father Marlo and Father Frazetti to meet her in Sydney."

"What should they do once she arrives?" asked Reno.

"Get her in private and convince her to join us. If she refuses, terminate her with extreme prejudice," answered Marzano.

"Yes sir," said Reno.

"What about Interpol and Equinox?" asked Marzano.

"We are unaware of their status at the moment, sir," answered Reno.

"For the moment, ignore them. I want to focus on Costello," said Marzano. "As for Equinox, we'll deal with them if necessary."

Simultaneously, on Sankan Island in the Triad's building, Deng was sitting in his office, having just been updated about Siobhan by his assistant Mazin. Deng smiled satisfied at the news.

"Fortune has smiled upon us my friend, this is what we've been waiting for," said Deng.

"Our operatives took this picture of her as she was boarding the plane," said Mazin as he handed him a picture of Siobhan.

Deng raised an eyebrow as he studied the picture, "Why is she dressed like a nun?" asked Deng.

"We don't know; might be some kind of disguise," replied Mazin.

"Craziest disguise I've ever seen; then again, considering the stories I've heard about her it makes sense," said Deng as he handed the picture back to Mazin.

"We think someone else is watching her," said Mazin.

"Is it the Networc or that Interpol agent? What was his name? Mendelsohn?" asked Deng.

"The Networc is a possibility but this is too sloppy for them, and as for that Interpol agent, we haven't heard anything about him since he left for Malvara," said Mazin.

"I agree with you about the Networc, besides they don't get recruits this way and the hell with that Interpol agent, he's done his part," replied Deng.

"Shall we proceed with the plan?" asked Mazin.

"Absolutely, contact our operatives in Canberra and tell them to go to Sydney airport immediately. Once she arrives tranquilize her and terminate anyone that gets in their way."

"Then what?"

"Bring her here," answered Deng.

Mazin looked at Deng quizzically, "Here sir?"

"Yes here, I intend to recruit her personally," answered Deng somewhat annoyed.

"Sir! Not that I doubt your powers of negotiation, but what if she refuses?"

Deng leaned back in his chair, a sarcastic smirk growing on his face. "Mazin my friend, there are two things I've learned in life, that everyone, no matter what they tell themselves or who they are, has a price."

"And the second thing?"

Deng raised his hands off the armrest of his chair, "Don't worry, be happy," answered Deng before returning his hands to the chairs armrests.

"Right, wasn't that a song by Bob Marley?" asked Mazin.

"No, Bobby McFerrin," answered Deng.

Chapter 16

Smack Down in the Big Smoke

Siobhan arrived at Sydney airport late that night; she disembarked along with the rest of the passengers. She immediately walked across the terminal to book a flight to the Philippines.

From the moment, she exited the plane she was being surreptitiously watched by two Chinese men in suits, who were in reality agents of the Heise She Li Triad. One of the agents was about to approach her when a tall man in a black pea coat, pants and white shirt wearing black tea shade sunglasses and a clerical collar walked up behind her. "Good evening, Sister Costello." said the man.

Siobhan tensed up instantly as she heard her real name; she spun around, ready for anything to face the man. "You must be mistaken," said Siobhan; the man grinned at her attempt at deception. Could Interpol have found me so soon, she thought.

"I think we both know I'm not," said the man who had immediately, taken notice of her tensed posture. "Relax, Sister; my name is Father Marlo, I'm not here, to arrest you," he said.

"Then what are you here for?" Siobhan asked.

"I will tell you but not here, follow me if you wish to know," said Marlo as he turned to leave.

Sensing little choice and admittedly curious, Siobhan followed the man out of the airport. The two Chinese men followed them determined not to lose them, but also not to be spotted. Siobhan followed Marlo to a car in a parking garage. Standing next to the car was a man dressed just like Father Marlo.

The garage was dimly lit and empty, putting Siobhan in a nervous mood. Father Marlo walked up to the other man and they exchanged whispered words in Italian. Marlo then turned to face Siobhan.

"Sister Costello, this is Father Frazetti," gesturing to the other man. "We represent a rather unique Order within the Vatican, charged with eliminating any and all threats to Vatican City and the Holy Catholic Church," continued Father Marlo.

Siobhan suddenly remembered what Mother Lucrezia had said about Disciple 13 and realized these men could only be members. "I already have a good idea who you are, but what do you want with me?" asked Siobhan.

"You see the Lord's church faces a great many threats, we are the ones who end these threats, and we would like you to join our ranks," said Father Marlo.

"What do you say, will you join us or not?" Father Frazetti asked.

Siobhan thought carefully, Mother Lucrezia had warned her about them and she swore after leaving the IRA that she would never kill for someone else again. She had spent her life killing first for the freedom of a country that viewed her and her former comrades as terrorists. Then she killed to redeem herself for those sins by hunting down the criminals and terrorists that struck fear into the hearts of God's children. She looked the two men in their eyes, having made up her mind. Siobhan crossed her arms, looked them straight in the eyes, and said "No."

"Is that your final answer, Ms. Costello?" asked Father Marlo calmly.

"Yes," she replied.

"I see, well that is quite unfortunate," answered Father Frazetti.

"How?" asked Siobhan.

Father Frazetti sighed. "Because we have to kill you," he said calmly.

Before Siobhan could respond a Techno arms Mag 7 shotgun slid out of his sleeve.

Frazetti aimed it at her and she jumped behind a nearby car, narrowly avoiding getting shot. Father Marlo pulled a silenced Glock 17 pistol out of his jacket, aimed it at the car, and fired three whispered bullets at her that bounced off the car. Instinctively she reached into her coat for her pistol only to remember that her pistol and weapons were in her bag on the plane. Siobhan shrugged, jumped onto the roof of the car, and lunged feet first at Father Frazetti hitting him in the chest and knocking him to the ground. Sensing Father Marlo behind him Siobhan swung around and knocked him down with a kick.

Father Marlo jumped back up and threw a punch at Siobhan, which she dodged. As Siobhan dodged the blow, Father Marlo hit her in the stomach. Gasping for air, she began to realize these men were as highly trained as she was. Defiantly she ignored the pain in her stomach and tried to hit him in the face. He caught the blow, hit her in the stomach with his knee, and pinned her face first against the hood of their car. She struggled as much as she could to get free from his grip, but couldn't.

"My dear, you should have accepted the offer," said Father Frazetti as he picked up his gun and then stood up. He walked over to her and aimed his gun at her head.

"It's a shame, you would've made a perfect agent," said Father Frazetti.

As he put the gun against her head, Siobhan closed her eyes and asked herself, is this it? Have I come all this way just to die at the hands of agents of my own church?

"I know it's a cliché but I can't resist; any last words?" said Father Frazetti, his finger tightening on the trigger.

"Yeah, duck," yelled a voice from behind them.

Before any of them could react, there was a short whisper and Father Frazetti and Father Marlo fell to the floor, dead. Siobhan immediately jumped to her feet and spun around in a defensive pose to face her saviors. They were two Chinese men in black and white suits and black tea shade sunglasses. One of the men was holding a silenced pistol with barely visible smoke wafting out of the barrel.

"Who are you?" asked Siobhan.

"Our employer has a job offer for you," said one of the men.

"So did they," said Siobhan gesturing to the bodies of Father Frazetti and Father Marlo. "The answers the same: No," said Siobhan.

As she turned to walk away, she felt a sharp sting on the back of her neck. Instinctively she grabbed her neck but her arm wouldn't move; then her legs gave way beneath her and she fell on her back. One of the Chinese men walked over to her, holding a strange looking gun in his hand.

"I'm afraid we insist," he said grinning before Siobhan lapsed into unconsciousness.

Chapter 17

Breakfast in Bed

Siobhan awoke in a clean, spotless hotel room. For a minute, she wondered if she was in heaven but then she heard the barely audible hum of the air conditioner. Next to the bed was a table with her Bible on it, on the far end was a table with a chair in front of the only window. She noticed her suitcase next to the bed and that her newly cleaned nun's habit was hanging in the closet, its door open. Suddenly she realized she was naked and got out of the bed and quickly got dressed.

As she put on her necklace, she tried to figure out what to do next. Suddenly a voice from a speaker on the ceiling chimed in with an answer.

"Welcome to Sankan Island, Sister Costello, we apologize for any discomfort, we have prepared a delicious breakfast for you," said the voice.

Siobhan looked around for the breakfast that was spoken of, and saw it sitting on the table. Siobhan sat down to study the breakfast; it consisted of toast, bacon, and fruit with coffee. She was about to begin eating when it occurred to her that it might be drugged. She brushed the thought aside, since whoever these people were, they would not have gone to such extremes merely to kill her, and she began eating; she was surprised at how hungry she was. When she was done eating, she opened the curtains of the window and looked out at the city below.

The only other building as tall as the skyscraper she was in was an equally large skyscraper across the street. The two buildings were surrounded by a ring of ghettos and slums. Beyond the city was a forest and what appeared to be a small mountain range beyond that. The whole island looked tranquil in the morning sunlight.

"So this is Sankan?" she muttered.

"Did you enjoy the breakfast, Sister Costello?" asked the intercom voice, interrupting her study of the city.

"Yes, who are you?" asked Siobhan annoyed.

"Leave your room and take the elevator to floor 102 and all will be revealed. Do not try to escape," said the voice.

Sensing little recourse, she shrugged her shoulders and walked out of the room. Then she walked down the hall and into an elevator, pushed the button labeled 102 and the elevator doors closed in front of her. When the elevator doors opened, again she was facing a hallway. At the end of the hallway were two large Chinese men dressed in black suits holding assault rifles standing in front of a large wooden door. Siobhan approached the two men expecting a fight.

But to her surprise they stepped to the side and opened the door for her. Siobhan walked in to see a man sitting at a desk, with his back to her, looking out at the city below him. When the doors closed behind Siobhan, the man began to speak.

"You know a person dressed like you is out of place in a city like this," said the man. She could hear a hint of sarcasm in his tone.

"Probably, who are you?" inquired Siobhan, annoyed at having to repeat herself.

The man spun the chair around to face Siobhan. "Sit down, Sister Costello," he said gesturing to a chair in front of his desk.

Cautiously, Siobhan walked towards the desk and sat down. "My name is Deng I've been instructed by my superiors to find you and I must say you've certainly made it difficult," said Deng.

"It depends on who's looking," Siobhan replied flatly, at which Deng laughed softly. "Who do you work for?" she asked.

"If you read the papers or watch the news, then you will occasionally hear our name mentioned. We are known as The Heise She Li Triad," he answered.

Siobhan had heard their name occasionally when she was in the IRA. "I've heard of you, you're some kind of mafia, right?" Siobhan replied.

"That's one way of putting it," answered Deng.

Siobhan's skin crawled in revulsion at his answer; even when she was in the IRA, she hated criminals like this man and his organization.

"However before we continue, I would like to apologize for the rather forceful method by which we recruited you, but we couldn't risk your refusal," continued Deng.

"Whatever you want me for, my answer is No," said Siobhan sternly.

Deng sighed. "And here I thought Americans were the only ones that cut to the chase. Sister Costello, let's be frank, you don't know what we need you for and to be honest, you kind of owe us."

"Owe you? How?" said Siobhan.

"Have you ever heard the saying that if you save a life then that life belongs to you," asked Deng rhetorically.

"It was you people that saved me in Sydney," Siobhan realized.

Deng leaned back in his chair and held up his hands with a sly smile. "Guilty as charged."

As much as Siobhan hated to admit it, he was right; she did owe Deng and the Triad for saving her. What made her nervous was? How was she supposed to pay them back?

"You've made your point; what do I have to do to make us even?" asked Siobhan feeling outmaneuvered.

"I knew you'd come around," he said with a sly grin. "We are assembling a team composed of...soldiers of fortune like you," said Deng smugly. "We'd like you to join this team. Once you and the team have accomplished that mission, we will be even and you may leave," he explained.

She was surprised at his answer, expecting him to have her kill someone or steal something. "What are we supposed to do specifically?" asked Siobhan.

"To find and kill the leader of The Networc," answered Deng.

Siobhan remembered hearing rumors of such an organization but chose to ignore them as the rumors they were. "The Networc doesn't exist," she said bluntly.

Deng's eyes suddenly took on a deadly serious glare to them. "That's what they want you to think. Anyway, you'll learn more about them at a time of our choosing," continued Deng, sensing her curiosity.

"When do I meet the other members of this team?" Siobhan inquired.

"Not for three months, the field leader is currently in the Middle East and we have yet to contact the third and final member," answered Deng.

"Three months? What am I supposed to do for three months?"

"We have several jobs you could do for us that require your skills, so do we have a deal?" Deng stood up and extended his hand.

Siobhan looked at his hand and weighed her options; she shook her head realizing she had none. "Yes" said Siobhan as she stood up and shook his hand. As she did so, Siobhan couldn't help but feel like she was making a deal with the devil.

As she prepared to leave, an idea suddenly occurred to her, "Deng, there's a large number of poor people in this city yes?" asked Siobhan.

Deng looked perplexed by the question as he leaned back in his chair.

"Yes there are, we provide the population with food and supplies from kitchens across the city," replied Deng, curious to see what she was getting at.

"Then can I work at one of those kitchens until you need me," asked Siobhan.

Deng laughed, "Clearly you're taking this whole nun thing too seriously, but I don't see why not," replied Deng.

"Thank you. I'll start tonight, but what do you mean by "nun thing?" asked Siobhan.

"You mean it's not a disguise?" Deng asked surprised.

"No, I became a member of the church after leaving the IRA," replied Siobhan straight faced.

"Now I've heard everything, I'll notify our people at the kitchens that you're coming," replied Deng.

"Thank you," replied Siobhan before walking out of the office.

As she walked to the elevator, she felt elated that she could do some good for the unfortunates of the city and that she would be able to punish the guilty while working for the Triad when they called upon her.

Chapter 18

From One Hand to the Other

Barry Mendelsohn was not in a good mood, after spending days convalescing in a hospital in Columbia. He had been recalled to Interpol headquarters in Lyon France, probably to be chewed out by Lohman for failing to catch Siobhan. He drove straight to Lohman's office, dreading the meeting with every footstep. He knocked on the door and entered. Lohman was sitting at his desk reading some papers.

"Sit down, Barry," said Lohman still reading the papers.

Mendelsohn sat down as Lohman took off his glasses, put the papers on the desk, and looked at him.

"Sir, I can explain," Mendelsohn began.

"Stop, you don't have to explain," interrupted Lohman. "I read your report and I understand what happened, but it's out of our hands now anyway," he continued.

"What do you mean out of our hands?" asked Mendelsohn surprised.

"I received a call from British intelligence several days ago; they're going to be handling the case from now on," he answered.

Barry could tell from the look on Lohman's face that he didn't like this development either. "I see, so what now?" asked Mendelsohn slightly relieved.

"For you, two weeks mandatory leave," answered Lohman.

Mendelsohn was shocked. "But sir, I know I can find her," he protested.

"Yes I'm sure you think you can, but the Brits are better equipped than us; besides her trail has gone cold," answered Lohman.

"What do you mean gone cold?"

"She was spotted arriving at Sydney airport in Australia. She was approached by two unidentified men and then disappeared."

"What about these two unidentified men?"

"They were found dead in the airport-parking garage, the only thing we found of Siobhan's was some blood," explained Lohman.

"She could be anywhere by now," muttered Mendelsohn as he leaned back in the chair.

"And she probably is but I want you to rest up. Anyway I've got another mission for you coming up," said Lohman.

"What's this new assignment?" asked Mendelsohn with a shrug.

"I'll tell you when you're back in fighting shape, understand?" said Lohman sternly.

"Yes sir," answered Mendelsohn, the words like ash in Mendelsohn's mouth. He hated having this case taken from him and replaced with something else, and he hated not getting his chance for payback even more.

"Good, dismissed," said Lohman as he picked up the papers and resumed reading.

Mendelsohn walked out of the office and back to his rental car. Once in his car he slammed his fist on the dashboard in anger, frustrated at his run of bad luck. As his rage subsided, he looked out the window and started the car.

"The bitch is probably laughing at me right now," muttered Mendelsohn. As he sat in the car, he silently vowed that somehow some way he would find her and bring her in.

*****

Felix Proffer sat in his office below the Thames in London patiently awaiting Nigel Solo's arrival. In front of him on his desk sat a folder with the letters L.A.T. stamped on it in red bold capital letters. Nigel walked in dressed in his grey business suit. The stern look on Proffer's face told Nigel all he needed to know. He sat down in the chair in front of Felix's desk and spotted the manila folder on the desk. Nigel had undergone several L.A.T. missions in his time with Equinox.

L.A.T. was a code for Locate and Terminate; usually missions like this were given to senior Equinox field agents. Felix never gave them lightly and his agents never treated them lightly. Nigel had a good idea who the L.A.T order was for.

"I'm a man of my word, Nigel," said Felix as he handed the folder to Nigel. Nigel skimmed through the folder, his suspicions confirmed.

"Let me guess: Interpol's agent found her and she killed him?" Nigel surmised.

"Close, the agent lived and they agreed to let us have it," answered Felix.

"That's surprising, I guess the Devil Woman is slipping," grunted Nigel dismissively.

"Either way, since Interpol botched it, the PM gave us an L.A.T. order on Costello. It's a standard L.A.T. order, find her, and put her down on sight," explained Felix.

"I'm looking forward to it sir, her and I have a score to settle," said Nigel smugly.

"I'm sure you are, but you have to find her first," said Felix.

"That goes without saying, sir," said Nigel wryly.

"Quite," Felix replied.

"So what do we have on her?" asked Nigel.

"She was kidnapped in Australia and we've lost all traces of her since. However, that file contains all the intelligence Interpol managed to get on her."

"So how do I find her then?" Nigel asked curiously.

"Now that we know she's alive we will be watching for her. When we find something you will be notified forthwith," answered Felix.

"So what am I supposed to do in the meantime?" muttered Nigel annoyed.

"Be patient SABRE, when we hear something about her you will be sent to investigate forthwith," replied Felix.

"Now, you're dismissed," said Felix. Nigel stood up and walked to the door, holding the folder tightly in his hand.

"Agent Solo, one more thing," said Felix just as Nigel placed his hand on the door handle.

Nigel turned around expecting to hear Felix say something along with the lines of good luck, however, the look on his face indicated otherwise.

"When this is over I don't want to ever hear the names Devil Woman or Siobhan Costello again in this office, am I clear?" asked Felix, his face as stern and cold as death.

"Yes sir," said Nigel before walking out of the office.

Chapter 19

Two down one to go

At that moment on the other side of the world on Sankan Island, Siobhan was in her hotel room in the Triad's building. She had returned there after working for six hours at a soup kitchen run by the Triad. She was kneeling in front of her bed resting her arms on the bed; she closed her eyes and prayed.

"Dear Lord, thank you for blessing me with this new purpose and watching over me as I repay my debt to these people."

When she had finished praying she undressed, showered and went to bed. On the top floor of the building, Deng was sitting in his office looking out the window enjoying the sunset, when Mazin walked in.

"Deng, I have to congratulate you on this whole thing with Costello," began Mazin.

"But" interrupted Deng knowing a question was coming.

"But sir, this whole thing about letting her work at the kitchens…?" said Mazin.

Deng spun around to face Mazin. "What about it? I've got her under heavy security and it keeps her on the island; besides it's not hurting us," replied Deng.

"What about the Vasilev Syndicate, if it turns out there's a price on her head? What if they try to cash it in?" Mazin protested.

"Mazin, the Russians know better than to interfere with us," explained Deng.

"True, but her story about quitting the IRA and becoming a nun, it sounds like a movie," Mazin replied.

"I'd watch it," grunted Deng sarcastically.

"Yes well, I just find it hard to believe that one of the deadliest women on the planet is a nun that just spent the night working at one of our soup kitchens."

"That could be the sequel," Deng said dryly.

"I don't think the Mountain Master would enjoy it," argued Mazin.

"Then we make sure that doesn't happen," replied Deng. "Anyway, now that we've found Siobhan, has there been any word about MAGIC 44?"

"Unfortunately no, though we do know he's not in New York, since we've already sent several people to his penthouse and he wasn't there," answered Mazin.

"And he still hasn't answered his phone?"

"Yes, we contacted the guild and according to them he's on a job," Mazin answered.

"I see, well we have to find him ASAP. Perhaps I'll go there personally and recruit him," answered Deng.

"It's an idea, but I'm not sure it's a good idea," replied Mazin.

"It doesn't matter now anyway since we don't know where he is…yet," said Deng.

"Right, yet," replied Mazin sarcastically.

"Is that everything, Mazin?"

"Yes," said Mazin as he turned to leave.

Once Mazin left, Deng swung the chair around, leaned back and looked out at the city.

"I am the king," muttered Deng as the sun descended lower in the sky.

The recruitment drive continues in Book four of the Shadow World: Death Dealers Incorporated...

About the Author

Robert Fisher was born in Long Branch, New Jersey. While attending Indian River State College, he began writing as a hobby that quickly turned into a passion for storytelling. After graduating from college, he sought to have his work published. He can be contacted on Facebook and Twitter at @ShadowWorld19. Hell to Pay is his third book. If you enjoyed it, get ready, because the best is yet to come...

Official Website of Shadow World Series
shadowworld96180901.wordpress.com

Other Books by Robert Fisher